BARE WITNESS

Collected Works

JOSEPH SMALL

Bare Witness

Cover Photograph by Joseph Small
Author's Photograph by Connal Small

Tellwell Talent
www.tellwell.ca

ISBN
978-0-2288-8980-9 (Hardcover)
978-0-2288-8979-3 (Paperback)
978-0-2288-8981-6 (eBook)

Dedication

This book is dedicated to my wife Connal

Golden leaves shake on dark limbs
Wind-scattered to earth
Where memory casts my heart

Mountain paths lead to bright moon
Autumn sky aglow
The restless road makes circles

You that single guiding star
Warm breath in cold bed
Amid this rattling house of sticks

Acknowledgements

I want to thank Sarah McGrath who generously contributed great effort to the development of the book. Her insightful feedback, editorial skills and assistance with poem selection were invaluable and greatly appreciated.

I also want to thank my lovely wife Connal for whom this book is dedicated. She has loved, nurtured and supported me, easing my way through life's journey in innumerable ways. Her strength is an inspiration. Her presence in my life my great blessing.

Finally, I want to thank the many poets, writers, philosophers, artists, teachers and all those influences that have colored my world.

Table of Contents

LOVE

AWARENESS

ANGER

HOPE

FANCIFUL

HOMAGE

LIFE

LIVE

TRANSIENCE

Preface

The poems contained in this book have been written over a span of nearly 50 years. They reflect observations on the comedy and tragedy of the human experience amid the miracle and mystery of our existence in this ever-fascinating universe. These are poems of life and love, anger and hope, humor and passing. The book is divided into nine categories, although certain poems could exist in multiple categories. Our lives are multifaceted and these poems attempt to capture the highs and lows, frailty and challenge of our daily encounter with life. My hope is that this poetic journey will resonate with readers and provide sustenance and a kindred spirit from a fellow traveler.

LOVE

Yes There Was Love

Yes this long road
Like a gnarled tree
Leaves to the four corners

Yes a path of joy
Winged soaring and joyous laughter
Skin aglow
Hands shaking with excitement
A wild vibration of cells
Blended existence
Great fling of life

Yes a path of sorrow
A love hurt deep as the burning of a branded heart
A restricted, feral, screaming
Like a baby stillborn

Yes a path of accomplishment
Rising beyond the imagined road
To paths and heights
And a precarious climb beyond all reckoning

Yes a path of disappointment
What I wanted
What I wanted
What I got
The ideal such a chasm

Yes there was fear
Dusk and foul paths
Shaking with trepidation
Holding back
Doubt and doubt and doubt
A sinking ruin

The endview from here is just fascination
All intent forgone to the accidental
Nestled in a cobbled and fictional narrative
Fanciful overlay

What merit or blame lays strewn
Gone into a winter's sky
But, yes, there was love!

Restraint of Trade

So much city to share
So much world—
Police barricades and peace demonstrators
Premieres
Assiduous after-dark worker bees
Pathetic in their metal and glass honeycombs.
The president in town
In this worn war-torn time.
Girls with umbrellas clad in shiny plastic coats
And sophisticated persona
That makes me want to know them
And then what…

All take meaning in your presence.
Maybe someday we will join.
You my muse of sappy, overly-pedestrian, word-ridden writing.

Some soprano sings bididee beep bop bow boo.
Tony Bennet strolls by, New York style,
One hand in pocket, other hand dancing
Some reggae, ballad-inspired rhythm of romantic loser awareness.
Sings, "Set em up Joe. Got a little story you ought to know."

Please don't think me pathetic with my star-crossed desires
Like some Shakespearean hero doomed to death.
Could you be some need I need fulfilled—
A beautiful, spirited, love-filled and generous
Beatrice from some ideal dream in my riddled mind?

Why don't I pursue you aggressively?

This world is too large and wonderful—
You too inviting for peace.
You urge my scrapper soul to search for yours.
Let's not discuss details of work or anecdotes
Or even parables.

Let us gather ourselves together and implode
In a belly-to-belly, direct hit, spirit-to-spirit,
Found-each-other, cloud-floating, surrounding-and-beyond-the-world,
Joyous, yea-yea-yea, boogy-boogy-boogy, giggle-giggle-gaggle
Encounter that includes all the freest best of you and me!

I sit on a fence and dream of you
Tumble tumble tumble all around.
You melt into me like quicksilver love.
We wish across the river at each other
And wave good-bye.

Love Wants

Pool of love restrained
Tame and idle laps
But should crash in waves seeking

I am the shoreline
White waves strong caress
Or lap with soft seduction

The tide soared out wild
Like the time under the white moon
When you said yes!

Aye I Wanted Her

Aye I wanted her
That much tis true
But only because I loved her
Through and through

Eyes round and sparkled
As fine China plates
Lips red as ruby
Almost gives me the shakes

Her skin shown as gold
But darker and richer
Beauty so precious
Could I be so bold?

To approach her was madness
With my poorly lot
Dim prospects and soul scuffs
How could I be enough?

Even more beauty
Inside than out
She nestled me close
Me a bedraggled old lout

Alas there was love
For me that's for sure
She also loved all
Who needed a cure
But I live with it gladly

Happy to be
Set free in her presence
This great feast for the senses
She shines a bright beacon
Always there to be seen
As I navigate rough waters
Through the sea that is me

Urgent Passes

I—Now
I grow great on your love
Like unexpected flowers from the sky
Or man-made weighty, meaningful geometric music
Or a field of green grass playing hypnotic vegetable melodies
Or trees exchanging leaves-across-the-sky, inner-earth, carnal whisper messages.

Your expansive sky-blue love shakes my Dante-like middle-aged lost center.
Like a turned-on Beatrice love with good-time physical harmonies,
Make me think I'm a body in a spirit and not otherwise.

Your love lunges at me with modern-day-dilemma insistence…
A semi-truck rolling out of control at me with too-late-to-avoid, *"What-is-this-commitment?"* veracity…
A sublime bandage for my invaded spirit.
It's-just-you-and-yet-you equals so much paradoxical power.

You make me love you cellular.
My belly reaches for you.
My buttocks embrace you with animal wonder.
You smell my desires.
My molecules tend towards yours.
Geese longing south know my feelings.
I urge you to me.

II—Later
Worship me.
Plague me with your wanton unrequited desire.
Make me itch with your want.
Grow hearts to be shunned by my anti-you fixed will.

I repel your wishes with the audacity of a flamboyant quill pen.
You are an unstrung puppet.
A plight. A schmuck in a photograph.
An emotional ringer.
A sweetheart sucker.
A moment lost.
An ungiving breast.
A denurturing duck.
A sensual shoeshine.
A dead John Doe.
A moment forgotten.
A passive hurt.
A dream unfurled.
A past atrocity forgotten.
A part of me ignored.
An urgent pass!

In That Infinity of Love

There is a vast magic in your eyes
Like so many universes
Mysteries that can never be unwound

How many hours have I stared into this starry realm
Gateways to a musing delight
Beyond all reason

My light is drawn into yours
Reaches through and pours itself
A river of delight and rushing current

There is no chance I shall be emptied
And every hope that you will be filled
In that infinity of love

One Beating Heart

When we were together
Every thought was right
When we were together
The stars released their light.

When we were together,
Romance filled the air
When we were together
Everything seemed fair.

And we were standing in the moonlight
Our shadows on the wall
Two thoughts evolved completely
Into one beating heart.

This is a moment for recalling
Tender spirit and flushed skin
When we danced the love ecstatic
And let each other in.

And we were standing in the moonlight
Our shadows on the walls
Two thoughts evolved completely
Into one beating heart.

Stroke

I am there beyond movement and speech
My soul vibrates beyond my stillness
My heart beats with love

My spirit is not caged
This incapacity does not still my way
Why do you look on me with sadness

My flight may flutter into the future
There is doubt in my faculties
But my love rises to embrace you
Your love sends me heavenward

There is only light
Light into light
Me into you

Just You and Me

Our breast we share so nicely
    should be held up as an example
        to all.
Yes! Our breast—a buoy
    keeps us afloat, safe
        from the undercurrent.

Beware the August green, that plague
    of barbed wire and lookout towers.
        Our relationship measured by firepower.
East/West machine guns apart.

Let us share the chores
    and eggs. Tree toilets for you
        and me. We'll share love
in October moonbeams.

Locked in a quixotic prison, we
    Stand up me back to yours. You
        East, me West. Surrounded by green.
Our prison rises from earth to sky.

Caught in a tree. Bound
    in roots. All
        my cares gone. The
peace of ashes.

With all the force of the beach
    receiving the ocean I
        linger in the moonlight.

This my first night in Peoria. Moon
    Shining half full, car
        door slams. Southern accents
couched in politeness.

The palms sing their silent psalms
    of fire, moon and ocean
        redemption meeting nihilism.

It dazzles, the ecstasy of being alive. Screaming
    "Who are you wondrous growth? A surprising
        noise snapping your fingers, breathing
your air, book opened face down?"
An Indian chant steady heartbeat
    beat beat. Drama has the Egyptian queen
        using feminine charms to enslave
the noble Julius Caesar.

Remember the beast…
    at dinner, during sex, at the hospital,
        while working, combing hair, wasting…
Remember the beast in refined tones over cocktails.

Bind the head for distortion. Hear
    the blood-sea sound in the shell. Shun
        the citizens from outside. Listen
intently to ancient seeds.

I am an idealist with no hope. Ripe
    full red lips are your style. Full
        black beard. The rhythm
of your right hand makes me smile.

So many possibilities caught in one fragile life.
Millions of births caught in a single frame.
Animated clay caught in a fog. Who
knows the shape of the lost-poem beast?

Dumb clay. Millions of it.
Keeps coming immense, terrifying and dumb.
A straight dumb line drive.

Fuck off all of you I love you.

Our Love

More than 15,000 nights we have lain
Mostly love
Always a conjunction of our spirits
Deep drinking at the trough of our lives
Love that binds in sweetness
Nurtured in experience
Our souls are bound
One to t'other
Tethered, tough no matter heartsick
Grounded in a single root
What great blossoming of beauty
Rises
Testament to a simple love story
That carried us across the rough tides of time
Divine and transcendent
You and me baby!
A great flowering!

Letter From an Admirer

This is my oblique way of overtly expressing my covert thoughts of you.

Think I'll give it all up to become your doorman. Get to greet you every day, *"Morning there, it's a beautiful day."* Maybe hum a few bars of *There's a Place For Us* before giving you a last long hound-dog love-lost look as you walk onto the elevator.

Or maybe I can survive with a long-distance woo of you.

Or just imagine my schoolboy love into a forged and fired, muscular and flexible bond with you. You and I naked under raincoats. Every cell erect and full of longing. We throw off our coats wet and wild, skin-to-skin, shin-to-shin, until we grow old with smiles from our many moments together.

It's not their fault but no one else can be you.

In me there's a voice that says, *"I want you as my partner."* Then, a part that calls that voice a betrayal says, "Hold back." It's like a frantic perusal with the brake on the floor.

You are a roller coaster I long to ride in every way. Yet, I stand with my ticket and gaze impatiently at the screaming excitement hoping, and fearing, I'll be drawn. The old pilgrim's lament: Two dead ends, splashed with remorse, and you still have to choose. What a wonderful and compelling predicament. My me wants to embrace your you in a transcendent dance beyond the shadow of reality where free spirits hug in unguilty ecstasy.

You deserve to be blessed by some soul of great stature and catching giggles and snuggly warm love in clear picnic air and hot florescent, say-blowing, blue-light, burning surging, libidinal-draining, all-out, caring, nighttime and daytime and even hard-time devoted love.

But, even now, my dream remains to tantalize—though I cannot eat!

Wild Love

I had a woman once
Daughter of the blue sky
Wastrel of the wanton
A deep way into the wilderness

She said,
This land does not belong to you
Never will
It is only giving that will make you whole

Clouds are but a dream
To the long mind of the land
Life but a passing shape sculpted in the ethos

Eros is all you need

Strike out into vast love
Give it all you can
Even to your last strength

Sweet Dreams II

Good night I am tired
Red roses close behind my eyeballs.
Somewhere a soft tide whispers tomorrow
And a sleeping struggle awakes into action.

Why the sorrow that floats like a thin film
In dank hotel rooms, houseguests of rage
Who slam the shades a million times a night
On the creeping bright lights?

Who could withstand the fascination
Of seemingly limitless fetid entanglements
Or ignore the heartbreak
That glistens like a bright light around our love?

How strange you stranger
Living here with me in confused love
Who shares our shaded view
As we gather into ourselves with separate fury

Unlock This White Room

A wisp of smoke rises—
No, it's your ashes

The energy of your tenderness
Blooms in my mind

Cuts me like the discovery
Of a forgotten love letter

Brings back the pain
Of missed togetherness

Alone surrounds me
A grove of bare trees

A room full of twittering yackers
Disguise their loneliness
Behind meaningless talking

May the wind carry you home
And my spirit find you there

Young Love

Now to live on recall
Those magic moments of love
When your heart lit up
Into glow and passion
Blending our two energies
Into one vibration
Rhythm of sweet joy
Supple youth
A summer sun of dancing light and cool shadow
Fresh morning wisps and muscle
Sheer exchange of want and gratitude
On the cutting edge of each moment
Now remembered well.

Beat Truth At Dawn

Early morning darkness
Clings to black trees.
Shadows blanket hard earth.
Winter brings the silent call of the birds
Distant, south and gone.

You reach across the bed
To the absent figure of your lost love.
Your movements shaky, old and abandoned.

All the promise of the day
Rises and moves
To some other place.

Enough to Light Our Way

Do not try too hard to look for meaning
It does not exist
But moments like sunrises
These are to be enjoyed

Rare and beautiful as birds in flight
Your presence soars
Against a brilliant blue sky

Sparkling seas contain your vastness

You have walked this path with me
And moved on to your own trails
Your presence resonates in empty places that fill me

There is a wonder we have shared
Dazzling and quiet as the stars
Shining in passing
Enough to light our way.

Don't Go

This tune my frock.
You sing it.
You sing it.

While Waiting

Wait
Stare
At the busy sky
With me

Listen in
Completely
Tuned into sound

Bend together
We become round form
We change
Things happen
Events
A history grows

Open yourself to me
You loud tacky form
Or delicate as warm mist on a cool night

Pass yourself around me
We change
Rise
And wait
An ever balloon of loss
Growing bigger

Goombay Ya

don't make my moment too long
I scream left and right
nobody says "too bad"
for measly one of six billion

Give me just enough action
to make a self-satisfied nun
smile
her unadulterated blue eyes
on round stiff breasts
screaming innocent desire

or

enough movement
to release a forgotten personality
lost by the death of a close friend

or

to dislodge a thought that won't leave

I
eyes closed
wish a tapestry
of secret sharing
between us
who find ourselves
justified by our moments of oh yeah

we swim the same waters
although varied currents make us cling
to varied moralities of I love you
some of which lasts
till our lips part
and we smile an eternal goodbye
no matter how goombay our lives together

Where Does Our Love Go

There the fire
Hot red embers
Love a twinkling of moon on a mountain river
Yes, our love lives in this moment.

A forbidden kiss does my soul wrong
I remember why my heart went this way
Love lingers in a midnight wavelength
Why does hurt cross our ways?

The sun gathers in a deep redness
Is it sunrise or sunset?
We go the way of the planets

We hang to our orbits
Find our way into the source
Where our love lies
A sweet burning to be felt.

Impossible Dream

There is only salt
        an attacking red knight
        and terror

Love one moment
        pure and sweet

Now a great missing
        empty air where warmth once embraced
        one beating heart where once were two
        mine captured, yours into an errant night

All quests fall like dead leaves
        into a deep wound
        wonder pooled at stagnant feet
        cold way and down the only direction
        my broken spear against the windmill of time

Grab Me Hard

There are many spots
Furthering my soul
For you to know all
Beyond the sparkle of me.

Several screams show
Naught of my anger
Nor disappointment
Etched in my cells of exchange.

Do not base your heart
On my quick waters
Nor my frail gone gifts
Like forgotten Christmas wrap.

Grab me hard and wait
My many visions.

Water Into Water

I cannot find my way into your heart without your help
Do not hide the path I seek to follow

It is a river that flows straight into love
If you are what you seek, I am love in abundance
Pouring out all around you

Please nestle into this watery sanctuary of warm desire
This wet sacrifice at the altar of the sweet heart

Jamaica in 1986 Dusk

So many dead things:
Calypso music
Beethoven
Halfmoon on the Atlantic
Sound of voices in pleasure
Moonlit midnight strolls
Saggy coconuts on brown palms
A rat on a cabana
The eager service
The indifferent
The foreign voice with its unknown promise
Restless leaves on foreign cement
The social freedom of white sand
The big dipper partly hidden
An understood glance

Yet, from my balcony I see:
A love car forever rolling
With two dreaming entwined
Belly-to-belly searching
Two ooh la las
Echoing in the evening
Two meanings bound for Mars!

Mirabai Says Love

Paleolithic lovers hug their soul in the quiet of the dark night
They utter into the sky

Neolithic lovers plant their seeds in hope
Happy in their unmoving domestic bliss
Walk familiar paths beneath a charted sky

Co-axial lovers radiate compassion to all
Align their embrace with universal forces
Seek a way to walk

Modern lovers give way to a frenetic pace
Seeking love inside of contraptions
Entwine themselves in separation

Mirabai says, "Love in all forms."

Refuge

The gray winds of winter blow
This pub alive with passing celebration
Conversations flow
Warmth and cozy wood paneling cast their comforting spell

Red and blue lights reflect off glass goblets, beer steins and brandy glasses
Forming shapes like metropolitan high rises at night

Heart beats of holy joy
Beat against my mind
Like a flock of wild doves loose in my head

Ghost and loss are exited in this moment
I smile into your eyes and say yes!

Resonate Way

It's hard to remember the many nights we had before

Sensual and sinuous in body and mind
Simple nights head on shoulder
Luminous explorations of skin and soul

Moonlight seeping through window blinds
Quick shadow racing across torso and thigh
Your heart beating fast against mine
Spirit seeking spirit amid the quick passing

Now
the giving away continues

In slow-paced walks
In memories carried
In simple assists of balance and movement
The dance no less elegant
The love deeper in every caring exchange
Love beyond wound
Membrane of heart wound ever tighter

AWARENESS

From the Bottom of My Heart

There is a poem at the bottom of my heart
I cannot express

Maybe something to do with age being a slippery slope
Or the privilege of joyous days gone by
Wrapped in the warm glow of the past like a halo over my memories

Or lost
Maybe it's some indecipherable Sanskrit writings
Erased and blurred on sheepskin parchment
A million times written over

Or core
Maybe it's hidden deep in the earth
Fiery and destructive
A molten lake bubbling with explosive energy
Searching through cratered layers for a way out

Or delicate
A small seed in late winter's ground
Waiting

Or spiritual
An island cathedral surrounded by tidal waters
With intermittent ways through
Like a distant radio signal that comes and goes

Or profound
A plunging into black depths that have no bottom
But may be a new way bridge
Beyond all mystery

Or perhaps creativity
Maybe energy moving ever outward
Racing into the nothingness at the edge of space
Bringing light into unchartered dark territories

Yes, there is a poem at the bottom of my heart
Resonant and orchestral
Not to be understood
That cannot completely understand
That cannot be said
But expansive
With all the echoes of the Big Bang beating

Sweet Dreams I

How many
draw the blankets
up at night
to dream
of unshackled zebras

The body released
in an eternity of action?

How many free
to dance
a pagan dance?
Free to find
intimacy in blood?
Being in the shape of breast?
The brown of nipple?

Wake.

Shun the strangers
who inhabit
your place at breakfast.
Their ways are not yours.
Their obese stomachs
evidence
of their will
to suppress you.

My battle lies
in my desire
to follow them
to the table,
to partake
of their blinding feast.

Heaven Scent

Feather me through this world
Wind a fine gold thread like the nuns used to say
My life, my gift

Prayer rises into the ethers
Like the rosy petals of sunrise
Abel burns wheat
The Greeks lamb

None as special as the dawning of the day
The rooster's crow is an awakening
Wipe the dreams from your eyes
See the burning that rises from the earth
Sad fire
Rising smoke of heaven thought

There are many colors in the wanting sacrifices
But no sure way to acceptance

The Long View

We are not there
Much sand between us and the ocean

The wilds of Africa stir my soul
The hyena in me loves the moon

I cannot reach the sky with my hand
The moon is too high to grasp
The stars invigorate my vision
The Milky Way fills my eyes

The path to the sea is blocked with distraction
Thousands of new moons darken the horizon
The sun sparkles and your pulse goes silent

Wake into a night of tall trees and deep roots
A lost lamp guides with dim light

Don't explain it's not your fault

Do not count on the sun in the sky
Or the earth s orbit
Or the ocean's tide

Rather find yourself in the leaves falling
The early morning mist
Red of sunset flashing on the horizon
The nights constellations

You are part of a larger tide
A crustacean of skin and bones
Muscles buried in wet sand

Puffy clouds are your way
Drifting in blue sky
Images of whales and flowers
Horses and crab
Sifting in the breeze

Set your navigation towards change
Your motions to motion
Your eyes toward an unfixed horizon

Eternity lies in the shifting sands
And the beating heart
Pale pulse of the frosty autumn grass
Whispering summer winds
Simply hold your love up to the sky and stare in wild wonder

And Sail On

I see my way to the sandy dune
Look out at a wild blue of movement
There is no rationality in those ebbs and flows

Soft clouds drift in an empty sky
Sailors on rough seas wave wildly to be seen
To be noticed on their precarious journeys
In uncharted waters

The hum that is heard resonates with awareness
But is not listening
Intent on dancing the infinite movement into moment
Passing like a storm cloud
Or sun dappled way

Do not look to the skies
Or turn your head to the past or future wake
Simply feel this vibration deep in your passing heart

There Are Stars in the Sky

You are not Socrates
Nor did you discover the bodies internal flow
Or the Earth's place in the heavens

Ode to Joy was a gift from the past
All You Need Is Love
A simple reverberation in your soul

Spring arises beyond your control
Harvest reaping waits not for you
Winter winds moan amid the thin embers of your waking
Deep snow of your being

Tide crashes against the slim bark of your striving
Your beached heart beats on the shore
Tired from casting

Mountains shrug you off like spring snow
A weary gravity keeps you earthbound

Clearly the willows are weeping for you
A lament of nature
Floral heartache, verdant despair

Where are you amid all this passing?
Just where you stand
Full of feeling and love and loss
Another forward movement
Crying mercy

The Vulnerable Given

The rediscovery of skin
chills me every time.

A cool pool.
That exact moment
of touch
a present-tense shiver
that stretches back to birth.

Or later,
that time of
rubbing your bubber,
your ass, and
wow a body…
nerves in a pocket of skin.

Out on the street
long days pass,
long tasks.
In dreams
I rise high
and light above
the world feeling
good! Soaring!

However,
my mighty roar of release
in this tiny bubble of skin
does not disturb the air.

Tough Love

Tough guys die too
Their locked hearts
And macho posing
Give way to time and fate

Generals, cops, motorcycle gangs
Mercenaries, thumb breakers and knuckle crackers
Presidential goon
All destined

Your muscle shirts are laughable
Your skeleton no more buffed than mine
Your vanity simple reflex
Nothing to the hard strength of time

So lay your thumb lightly on the scale
Your heavy weights are simple injustice
Reptilian ways
That lead us backwards
May the "Might makes right" be lost in the bone of your brains.

Double Star

O distant star brother
In distant space
Tell me bedtime stories
Of your passage
Into my bones and blood and tissue

Calcium, iron and carbon
What prodigious and fortune forces
Bagged my mind to exist of you
Beneath your watchfulness?

My eyes look up at you
We share a lonely moment on the beach
We wink like old friends with no need to talk

Like me, you are a bundle of energy
Trapped by gravity
A fluid of burning
Tethered by borders of space
Integral to your ontical perspective

Cover me as I go on my way.
I'll honor you like a bright son
Who loves you

Beauty Passing

Beauty is the scraping of my soul on my Mother's threshold.
The sun-bleached curtains that hide her heartache.

Beauty lies in the salted brass
Slow coloring of loss
Strong wind blows seed to fate

There is beauty in the raindrop drawing its dissolution across my windshield
Hieroglyphs to a silent sky

There are paths in the earth
Trodden ways
Where many have walked in the sun
A beauteous design of passing

Our marks are like scratches upon rock
Energized impressions of love and loss
Expressions of being resonating with meaning
Beauty there for our reading

Our loss accumulates into progress
Slow and unsteady
Shaky
But beautiful in its imagining

The Liquid Atmosphere

My social life is filled with chatter and presentations.
Our surfaces, like water—reflective on top
And deep with many forms of life.

The dark and furtive, the bright and joyous
In their expansive private reef.

There sits quiet
With something vast
Like the rustling leaves
Of a million underwater trees
On a soft summer day
With scant fluffy water clouds
Lilting breezes
And a breathing consciousness
Filling our gills.

But it is impolite to talk of it
Floating down there
Deep beneath our eyeballs
Like a distant mote.

Cloudy Perception

Close your left eye.
Put your thumb over the sun.
Switch eyes and the sun reappears.
Glasses on, eyes see the bright star.
Off, it blinks into nothingness.

Distant burnt-orange
Where hours ago the sun
Passed into the ocean's horizon.

The noise of waves as they
Dissipate into themselves.

My mind a receptor
For the senses.
Other signals land
Harmless and missed.

Stars form a wave
That is a dipper
That is a fabrication

I sense 10,000 things
But miss the infinite points
That blast out our existence
Like an unheard song.

Long Distance Calling

It's easy to feel
The creative force of existence,
Flashing manifestation,
When you're in Maui
At the Four Season's Hotel.

The wind born in Africa
Wafts up from the dust
From draught
In the form of a prayer.

And, through slow tortured birth
Begins its journey
Up into the highwinds
With the force of sacred air
And stretches out
Over the Pacific

Gathers energy and finds me
Here at the Grand Staircase
Invigorated from vacation rest
But burdened with
The meandering message
Of neglect and loss
And cold unconcern
And the dust of compassion
Vibrating like a cell phone.

Through A Train Window

Fleet chariot clouds leap towards brilliant orange
They dance muscular and true
Message of immensity
Sign of an invisible creator?

There's a moment when the sun sets to brightest red
And the sky loses its liddishness
Until you beg for relief of its setting
And the cool grayness of twilight.

Ancient powers of night emerge
To flex muscles once more
Amid junk heaps and shattered cars
Scattered like so many char-riddled stars.

The cubic shadow of a semi-truck
Shifts balls out
Black-hole comet through soft grey darkness
Like a fist or a pathetic, overstated display of power.

My spirit laughs
And glows its tiny volume
Like an answering son
On its way to the horizon.

Prayer for the Birds II

A flame of light
On each our forehead.

Eternal
We mingle in a furious blaze of power
Dancing flames to sacred melodies of liberation

Foul nature
Parasite of false life
Borders of skin
Cells in captive union
You have no power over me.

Do your worst and I
Buoyant love do smile
Of cloud and bird in flight and untethered
Levitated

Bow my humble flame to your altar
Pray forgiveness for my weight

Please do not choose the stump
Of my dancing spirit
Rather may that part of me which crucifies
Depart

May the springs of my joy
Like seasons everlasting
Or water overflowing
Ever venerate your sacred heart!

The Me Me Me Me Illusion

There is no one who ever knows you
Dante never knew Beatrice
Though he loved her
And look at you looking at me
You don't know me
Though you love me
What say you stranger to my stranger?
Never knew you
Never knew me
Though I love you
That's just my musings
Nothing to do with you
Don't hate me
Because you don't know me
Sunlight reflecting on water
That's you looking at me
There I am
Gone before you can see
Or a fairy tale for you to decipher
With no happy ending
Or see the moon
That is not me
My persona is Mr. Moon
There is no place where I am there
It is just me a floating awareness under the sun
Pointing my way towards me

Dance of the Trees

Wind dancers
Boogie woogie wigglers

Sublime with still movement
That whispers its way into our hearts

Wild seducers with bark fros waving
Against blue sky and white clouds

On grey days you still feel their vibrating ecstasy calling you
And how gorgeous in the snow
Against a slate-blue background

The silky movement of a thousand limbs
Wooded cymbals chiming out the beat

Wait for us there
We will come dance with you

Same Old Story

The Neanderthal shakes his fist at the sun
And so do I

The moon bedazzled us both
The same darkness lay at the bend of the path

We wish toward tomorrow
So many sparks in the night
It is the dreaming that flies to the stars
This we share.

A Proper Dwelling

The truth is you don't know what will kill you
So do not dwell on death

The rain falls heavy in the pre-dawn darkness
A shiver runs through the rain-soaked Parisian dawn

Dark aisle of Communion
The many earthen shuffling towards the divine
Golden glow distinguishable in the chill morning
It is a slow ritual movement

What mystery shines
Draws us forward
Step by step
Transcendent communion
Sacrifice of reason

Nurturing light of our minds
Glimmer of hope
While restless days pass

Make it a dance upon the rough waters
Divine hands folded towards the heavens
Imagining the sublime
Human submission to the powers of mystery

Meet Me In The Morning

I
Light flows out of me
Like liquid oozing
From wounds

As if I am
An unlucky bit player
In a badly made western

Stars shoot from my eyes
A haze clouds my vision
Like a polluted city at dawn

Gravity maintains my shape
As my energy is blown to the cosmos

Rocks shudder as I pass
Trees shiver and shed their leaves like tears

II
And so this unintended aberration
This birth of wrong
This compassion wasted
In horror and longing and misconceptions
And doubt
This bankruptcy of misspent time

This great bruise of waste
Waiting for deliverance
Inept and cut off from the great flow
Reaches out a trembling hand
And is grasped by the magnitude
Disappearing for a moment into a throbbing wave.

Fight or Flight

I sit safely on the sidelines
My muscles knotted
Killing me slowly
With survival response.

A table blooms on the balcony
Like a flat white plastic flower.
The chair that I sit on looks dignified
Full of energy.

My electrons whirl.
My magnetism gyrates.
My heart turns away
From the world like
A repressed peasant
Searching for invisibility.

My passions lie drowned
Heavy in a sea of my concern.

Tiny movements of fright
Tremble my perimeter.
My machine guns are on
And flailing.

The world takes shape
In my mind
And peace lies
Just beyond reach
Of my concepts.

The Great Delight

A walled enclosure of delight
Gigantic life-giving trees
Reach to the heavens
Vibrating with a slow and ancient majesty

Gnarled root and scarred bark
Studded with stars like radiant holiday bulbs painted by Van Gogh

You must climb high to reach for this celestial fruit
Which never has been grasped
But which is the only good thing worth aiming for

Head Trips

The stars make me feel like yesterday
They don't mean to

The light makes me feel like tomorrow
Does not mean to

This energy flowing through the cosmos crashes into me
Quite by accident

My heart beats on the horizon
Lost in sunshine
It don't mind

Seduction

No, it is endless

Charred trees
Forgotten dead
Barren waste

Patterns of ice in a cold world
Low sun on dead winter
Empty lands laid waste

Do not be fooled
When you look into the skies blue seduction
A simple containment

So too fields of flowers
An illusion to daze each generation
There is betrayal in every fallen petal

Shallow graves mark the landscape
They fall in every season.

The Sweet Gift

Children are encouraged to their ultimate selves
No one ever thinks only of themselves
God's sweet warmth musters our strength
And, to show our love, we'll go to great lengths

No furtive acts of abuse and bile
No overt threats of Nazi violence
No dignity-shattering shaming
No

Give me naivety
Naïve love
Naïve peace
Naïve romance beneath an apple tree

Don't rock and rip my perfect world

No covert institutional and dumb suffering
No murder, rape and scam
No apathetic humanity
No values of hatred and fear
No political corruption or fundamentalist religious oppression
No bribes or genocide
No heartless smiles

Don't upset everything that I hold dear
Just give me naivety.

Sitting Meditation

Shake your head
And the stars shimmer in the sky
Infinite space Afro, no boundaries to this noggin

Spin your being
Light reaching out into virgin space
Mind ever expanding

Comets race through your mind
Planets spin amid expansive thoughts
Enormous sound fills your ears

Arms and legs are galaxies
Vessels of dark energy
Light your blood

You come and go in ever changing form
Snapping in and out in a vibration of creation and destruction
A wave that moves through time

Don't put a veil between you and the universe
This illusion does not stand
Your heart beats in the far sky

Me Me Me Me

You stalk me.
Hurt me.
Mold me into lost
long-gone, sit-on-the-fence
"two-dead-ends-and-you-still-have-to-choose"
loser mentality.

How can I be happy?
Your hand holding grabs
me round the soul
like a star-lost light
sparkling like my young hopeful eyes.

Makes me think of innocence and adventure,
LSD, a car and a lonesome two-lane highway
in an old yellow Rambler from 1965
with a steering wheel the size of a bus,
my two hands like a three-year-old's
on a cosmic wheel with lethal consequences
to my pathetic destiny.

I spend my time like a spiritual sniper
shooting toward my space-time-continuum soul
murderously bent towards itself.
Why?

Don't laugh you overly-aggressive
self-centered foreigners of other cultures
who flock to others' ideas of the world.
I want to control you with my mind.
Guarantee myself the best seat in the house,
the best unadulterated ass,
the primo squeeze with angelic overtones.

Don't miss you, you miss me I want.
Contemplative interaction with life I want.
Sigh with spent relief I like. I say,
"Don't bother me with your coughs
and your heavy warts and bloodbath-scenario futures
of hapless physical fodder. Just
give me the best of all
sex and spirit and love everlasting."

Your circumstantial details,
sweat of existence,
don't inspire me.
Your "wither wills" don't attract my attention—leave
me ephemeral as a grace-filled thought
filtered through your purity
like an exclusive water of joy.

You come in like a rainstorm
with your change and pacifying, a giant cloud.
Yes, I worship a misty goddess and pray for protection
from a bright sun and my me-me-me-me world.

Vanity Rocks Your Boat

Yours is not the center of the earth
Yours is not the center of the universe
Yours is not that around which all revolves
Yours is not next to angels or select child of god
Yours is not just what you see but much more
Yours is not solely the domain of good

Algae and fish and monkey are you
Alive in the dark unknown of your mind
Animal lurks there of untold value
You are a lover of sex
A parasite of hunger
Imaginer of grandeur
Dreamer of a golden heaven

Just beyond your reach
But enticingly in your vision

The universe grows without you

The leviathan calls
Faceless
Unlistening
A brutal intelligence
A reverberation of power
Amid a darker, more profound ocean.

Vanity Takes a Bow

The feeble attempt draws me to my knees
All the meaningless movements
I try to aim for the sky

In the scheme just a dream

Odysseus on his voyage
Twenty years he did destroy
Home and family under strife
All the men after his wife

In the scheme just a dream

Our trials are our own
Everything goes its way
We are each just a stray

In the scheme just a dream

My heart soars towards an empty sky
I blow a kiss and wink an eye
Realizing in the end it is all goodbye

In the scheme just a dream

With this simple truth
Pray let go
Give up your power's thirsty flow
Lay down your arms
Turn on the charm!

Tit for Tat

This is just this
And that that
Where are you at?

Green is the grass
Red the rose
What that means I don't suppose

Water flows down
Air rises up
Be sure to drink fully from the cup

Wind blows high
Roots sink low
Keep on moving when you receive a blow

Life can be fancy
Life can be dull
The wonder exists mulling the mull

No Way to China

Shattered pieces of me
like a woeful, clichéd blue
clatter
as I walk
a moving disturbance
of unbalance.
Sharp pieces of me
hurt.
Sharp crystallized dust
weighs heavily
on my feet.
I am filling up
like a sand clock
with the indistinguishable
pieces of me:
beaches of mess
to dig and dig.

God Comes A Knockin

I feel God vibrating in my frontal lobe
Connecting me to a vast undulation
Trees, grass, earth, water, wind
Bodies, insects, birds, air
All a twittering.
Dance of creative energy
Or conscious matter.

The current flows through
Down my body
Across my limbs
Tickling me with an eternal glow
A movement that does not stop
An intelligent striving
Reaching out
Into unknown miracle.

A place to go.

Give Yourself a Hug

I am walking to you
From the stuff of me to the stuff of me
Separated from my own vibrations
The sweet hum we share

I fight through a thousand distractions
To discover that quiet voice
So soft and peaceful
Calm as a languid river
That winds itself slow
A pulse
A steady beat of life
That bustles us forward
Into our own waiting arms.

Courage of Gauguin

To find my courage, like Gauguin,
Would hurt so many.

I see my end
In a cheap hotel
Dreaming of what
Could never be.

Hold me close God
For I am a weak candle
Far from your image.

Besieged!

With all effective stratagems
Long proven futile.
I fall
Net gone
Defused of buoyancy
Victim of gravity

And sorry for my inevitable mistakes.

Ambient Light

So many nouns dancing their energy.
Each slim moment marked by each spent slim beam.
A rock, a leaf, all those wild yous of light!
Open shadow between mountain at night.

Does sent spark seem often sad SOS?
Or is it sad filter of me who sees
Certain "pathetique" in the evening breeze?
I have asked the question no one says.

I walk with fellow walker who asks too
If you, I, he, she or the immense it
Has long love that exists beyond the grip?
We mean does intellect answer cow's moo?

For frantic I talk to the stars who wink.
Is it folly then to assume one who thinks?

Prodigal Son

When I was a schoolboy,
I dreamed of being close to you.
"Please challenge me," I prayed.
I knew I could do it—
Conquer all evil.
Digest it like a poison overcome
By my plenty of antidote.

But the measure of your love
I now question
As my dull soul revolts me
With mediocrity and confusion
And self-hate and self-love.

Like all the talentless
I long for total freedom.
Leave me to my ineffective musings
And moral ineptitude
And courage-less existence.

I deal in ideals
Obsessions, yet,
Incapable of murder,
Scared of love,
Pathetic and passive,
I consume your blessings
With softy remorse.

My Great Disgrace

There goes the thought
The awful thing my mind has wrought
There goes the day
Another chance just thrown away

What chance is this
To say what means this passing bliss
Or the sorrow the day affords
There is no place I'm moving towards

Just gone and gone and gone again gone
That is the fate I'm moving on
To task to task not more alas
Not strange to realize nothing lasts

Where do they go
Where do they stray
As each the moments go away

Into a meaning gone to waste
A story once told

My great disgrace

Dharma Bum Blues

I am a beatnik pilgrim on the road to nowhere
Empty is where my soul does beat
Like Joyce said, "Daedalus paring my nails"
As times cruel passing slowly defeats

Sing me toward the morrow
Sweet nightingales bring on dawn
Sun rises toward my slow decay

Many years pass in my absence
Before and after

What aria cries my sadness?
What loss must be borne?

Colorado's mountains are not high enough
To soothe the morning's loss
Colorado's mountains are not heavy enough to cover my radiance

Majestic goes the ticking of the clock
Great heights
Great sighs
Great riddance

I turn towards San Francisco in hope
Searching for a poet's soul
And a simple happiness

Tap the Great Flower

The trees are alert to your vibration.
The mind sensitive to your attitude.
In spite of Descartes,
It is not all in your head.

Listen hard.
The great wisdom of consciousness
Buzzes like bees.
Those who are receptive
Need not worry.

The sweet nectar flows
For all to taste.
Turn your head toward sustenance!
Go gentle into that sweet joy.

What Say You

Say stay do not go
Or all your days be filled with woe
Do not walk the fell way
Travel instead to light of day

What harken waste does haunt your breath
What soothes the ache of a branded stealth

The scar protrusion dost label you
But this must not beholden you
Many the marks along the path
Are borne by skin and mental sash

Tis your decisions straight and true
That lead to your infinitude

When Peace Will Reign

When the leaves are sad in autumn
And the North wind slowly turning
And the daylight fading westward
All flowers petals falling

When my heart is planted firmly
In the soul rich with past
And the sky is glowing russet
Among the starry glory cast

I will rest my weary wandering
In the places of my mind
And peace will reign forever
In the orbit of all time

The Wow of the World

I tap onto consciousness
A tendril seeking in and out
Aware of the windows.

The panorama of snow and trees
And white rooftops.
The wool shirt on the chair back.

Paper and books flung about
Through chance and interest

Suddenly a great energy
Slaps me so hard
The world crumbles
Into magnificence.

ANGER

A Children's Gift

Then when they come
We'll take flight
Banish our fears and memories like fossils
Now step to the tall trees
Sway with the branches
Lurch skyward and descend
Is this Frost's birch?
The broken glass of heaven?
Then when they come
They will know
We were here by the ruin
Our monuments will leave painful scars
This dust
Is it pieces of hell?
Then when they come
They will come by the billions
Too many to sustain
It is good we will be gone
For they will have much to say of us
How could we let our illusions turn our heads?
Ashes fall and here they are
Now it is time to go
Leave your place in the tall trees
Turn your eyes from the blistering sky
Give up the cool breeze of your movement
Go back and find your place in the ruined ground.

Dreams into Nightmare~*Dedicated to Toni Morrison*

The grieving post runs south from here
Parallels a scorched path of ignorant hate
Trees fed on blood and scarred by rope
A phantom host born of dim horizon and pale insecurity
Vibrates in the twisted limbs

All the lost possibilities
All the loss
Dreams into nightmare
There is much to grieve.

Mark of Cain seared deep by countless cowardly actions
An original sin branded obscured by a white-washed gentility and unearned privilege

All the lost possibilities
All the loss
Dreams into nightmare
There is much to grieve.

Blind of justice ripped from her face to bind hands
Eyes askance to a jury-rigged verdict
Releases a revengeful band of Furies
Loose to the just winds of time

May they clear a broad road
So that grieving may find its way into all hearts
And the long hope of diversity
Raise the healing joy of enlightenment
And the power of unlimited possibility unleashed

Wild River Rolls

Where is the spirit that youth gives for free?

A wild river runs just below the surface
There goes your grandfather's timepiece
Your Dad's wing tipped shoes
Your first loves beating heart
Thousands of identities gone to Banana Republic policy

There is a deep darkness my feeble candle cannot penetrate
Selma and Memphis
Dallas and Los Angeles
Two mass shootings in the U. S every month
Idi Amin, George W, Assad, Pinochet…
So many wolves in the woods

Up here raindrops ripple the water's surface
October fills every space
Days get dark
Cold moves in like an angry mob

Buried in the deep
Waves roll over me
Distorted images of sun dance on the surface
Or is that the light of the moon?

All this fluid washes over me
Cleansing me of skin and muscle
Leaving me bones
Sticks floating in an unrelenting current

Night is yellow fog
Sulphur smell
Reminds me of my childhood

There I am praying as a child
White sports coat
Pure as grace
Thinking of the billion forms of life that have passed
Why am I so placid in my anger?

Are you sleeping
Are you sleeping
Row row row your dream gently down the stream

If you lose sight of the wild river
Look into their eyes

Famine

There's a moon set in deep twilight blue
Slow rise on the horizon.
A moment of fatted time and rich sacrifice from plenty.
Wine flows amid rich and sophisticated cuisine,
A treat for the eyes as well!

When painful stories follow moonrise
Indifference disguises itself
As sincere head shaking and tongue clucking
Like spared chickens to their headless sisters
Aimless scurry.

How goes monotonous, long-term suffering?
Tide ebbs for days and years.
Wet sands dry and deserts form.
Blood dries around bitter lips unnoticed.
Eyes stare heavenward and vacant.
What cursed deed equates to this?
What noble action can redeem?

Cattle and sheep long gone on an unnaturally quiet landscape.
A full moan rises into a wailing screech.
Rebellion surges against empty air.
Spirit walks to the table for a feast
And goes home hungry.

Broken

There are disasters on Main Street
Disasters in the lonely wilds
Disasters in between

Generation on generation
Fathers go their weary way with abandon
Children
Like flotsam
Damaged debris
Caught in wild currents
Anger in their veins
Loss in their hearts

Hurt breaks
Wave on wave
Ripples wide and damaging
This is no wonder
But the sad conveyance of rusty neglect

There is a sea of sadness growing ever deeper
Preying power devouring innocence
A rushing river that drowns

Wake Up

I
There beneath the tall cliffs
In the deep valley
The children hide

The heights are busy with discussion
Talk of climate and peace

II
But the river runs
Like a story through my heart
Rich with stirring heroes and brave daring
All eyes on the far windmill

Pure waters and green pastures
Rich abundance of nature
Peace in the valley of the Soul

There in the sun
There in the moon
There in the misty morn

See it in the star
Find it in the blue sky
Unfetter your wintery mind

What a swirl
What a whirl
What a mystery to divine

III
Yet here in the dark emanation
The children cower

All eyes turned inward
While the outside hurtles
A gravity of destruction

I've Been Egypted

I
Oh my eyes
Sore from imagining 1902
And the ravages
Of flooded Egyptian villages.
People chose death over exile.
Who can blame them?
Spontaneous vermin eruption
On that bread they were saving.
Unknown deadly diseases...
Polio, tuberculosis, tapeworm...
Utter lack of fish,
Flies aplenty.
And HOT!
With no sunglasses!

II
Even keeping clean not easy.
Plowing land hard.
A nation of farmers
And uneducated fishermen.
You can hear the sad pipes play
Like a PBS special

III
As we go about our daily necessities.
My bare feet know the earth well.
The great dust of my ancestors
Mixes with my breath.

IV
We embrace
Like two inconsequential facts.
We hug and exchange
The empty information of our lives.
We imagine ourselves more fertile.

V
I live in the tombs of my ancestors
With the polluted topographical perspective
Of modern life.
My slow alligator world accepts you
As you have accepted me.
Today's store-bought riches my due
Like the measure of my new-born soul
As I squeeze the trigger
On an American-made gun
And blow my image to Giza.

VI
I take my place in the millennium
A piece of dust in the sun
Unnoticed on my child's brow.

Irrationality

Springs from nowhere
Shoots out from repressed desires

Oh to be king
And worshiped
Admired

These flaws are not of your own doing
Brain takes over
Bruised blossoms grow from unfettered impulse

You see crowds in your mind
All in awe
Adoring acolytes
Glazed worship in their eyes
Fear in their hearts

You point them forward into a frenzy of hate
The enemy deftly sliced from humanity
Painted as other
All thought and emotion
Gathered away and targeted there
With the evil power of a lynch mob
An Artesian fountain of discord
And insatiable desire
Reverse alchemy
That turns all that is gold to lead

Hatred

A constant gleam in
a chicken's eye, a
precisely defined
white room, a
casual not-looking, a
total removal or lack
of imagination, you
are other, that is that, it doesn't matter
to me. Me is
Everything.

Hatred:
strolls down the
street unmolested,
conspires sitting
casually in over-
stuffed armchairs. Lives
in a gigantic antique
museum piece that
reminds us of our
greatness.

Hatred:
Implies unquestioned
agreement. The wheel
spins downward, the
rock pulls toward the
earth; the easy completion

of any movement. The
separation, my skin
against yours the limit
we share.

Fists of Rage

Waves crash over taut hands
like roving cliffs of danger.

Sinuous muscles round thumb
ripple with malice.

Skin, subtle shades of golden white,
like the soft-lit folds of renaissance robes--

The holy attire of medieval tyrants.

What power to do evil washes
like silt into the surrounding waters?

What subtle motion environs
so much danger, so much damage?

Each caress corrupts and pollutes
with insidious and invisible impunity.

Brute force subjects waters,
baptized with filthy intention,

Which struggle to maintain integrity,
to cling to innate nature,

And rise powerful, clenched
and ready to strike...

This moon-struck tide, this salty being,
this liquid soul

Angered, already defeated.

Oh El Salvador

Fifty deaths
in the sound
of a bird's wings.
How many
In a gone flock?

Wake me
in your movement
from hope.
Wake me
with your buried tongues,
with our over-satisfied smiles.
Wake me
with the simplicity
of your deaths…
my life an horizon
of your hopes.

I listen
to the sound
of your mother's spade
in the red earth
in the ritual
of burying your lost body.

Air fills your grave.
Reach out to me mentally.
Explain your lost substance.
Your southern earth
Your scattered Indian dust

lost beneath the righteous dollars
of the north—
lost in the round vowels
of forked English.

Yet Subject to Arrows and Rifles

Today I am a bison
Full of power and sinew
A stampede of energy
An animal locomotive

Today I bear an animal heart
Filled with beating sorrow
Proud with dignified life
Searching for companionship.

Today a deep well of life to share
Plenty and water in my dreams
Moisture and awareness in my eyes
Mother beneath my feet
Deep breath of ancestors fills my lungs

Many trails to run as I depart this place.

Worldly Ways

For now I can see the stars
Like bones in a dark sky
Skeleton of the universe
Dark flesh of space
Planet organs

But what deep and poisonous smog invades our atmosphere
This gray and sickening weather
Killer of thousands
Danger to all

Breath comes hard here
A deep hate calls the shots
1953 England and a Churchillian indifference
"Just the weather," he said

Fate can be so cruel at times
A conspiracy of dunces they say
Power trips in their reptilian heads
Divide and conquer they say

Coal burns in the city
Ignorance rules the day
This we must survive
Until the weather changes
And that someday sun rises

Seeds of fear grow in the imagination
An insidious evil of power
A dark side that hides behind a thin veneer
Just enough substance to appeal to provincial wrong-headed ideas

Search and you will find
A darkness hiding in the everyday
A projection that is not true
A way of being wrong

The Inescapable World of Color

Your race will make you act
This is wrong
But an understandable bias
You are alone within subsets

Our vision of togetherness is only a dream
Our hate is stronger than our love
But this is not the direction

Breeze blows
Sun shines
Yet we lose our way

The warrior does not need war paint
But the hearts of the settled ones to open in reckoning
With a recognition of the living power of land and wind and water
A release of the soul from reservation

The women and men of color
Survivors of sinful exploitation
Undaunted spirits
Proud dignity of perseverance

I will not lay this dye upon my skin
No disguise will hide me
My failed actions are my own

Sky is a long way from the earth where we lay
How do we find gold of rainbow?

There is black blood in the soil
Red paint in the sky
And a withered growth in a desolate landscape

Privilege

Contusion of hatred
This capital offense
Great fear of color
Skin abhorrence

Clinging to privilege
Desperately casting for caste supremacy
Imagined superiority
Loser's grasping
A democratic aneurysm
Grave injustice
Road to ruin

Cast off your misdirection
Your battering pales to theirs
Look to the jiggered system
The culpable brokers
Standing on promise

May tide crash towards love
In a tsunami thrombosis of passion
A vein that flows deep into our hearts

The Wide Western Skies Cry for Justice

These Native American voices sing into the afternoon sky
The wind rustles with a genocide of voices
There is chanting and dance amid the sorrow

Wild horse angry warrior attack
They beat and bloody you
Righteous in their anger

Great spirits join in the firmament
They know the past
And the paths of forked tongues
This is the way of the world

The crow in us caged
The wild entrapped

The arrogant empowered
Churn their dead souls into a flickering light
While casting us into darkness

Whisper this truth to all you meet
This breezy whispering cannot be ignored
How can we rise when so many are fallen?

Prophets Not Profits

The big dogs are on the prowl
Wolf howls reverberate in the twilight
Impalas invade Europe
Wild is on the rise

You
You begin to dance
Undulating fibers find release in your rhythm
Cells vibrate to erect and receiving

Trees shimmer in rich color
Alive with movement of leaf and twig
Make a subtle percussive beat
Sway in seductive moves that lead to sweet embrace and tender shoots

All awake to a wonder
Shining in the glow of force
That rises

Small gives way to the infinite
Pandora's box is thrown open
But only jewels emerge
All trapped good goes free

The heartache of confused differences
Manipulation
Exploitation
Slink off into the dark

A snake in the grass
With death on its mind

We gather round the fire
See each other for the first time
Banish the sinister energy eastward to the land of Nod.

Under the Spell of Wild Wonder

Look out!

The butterfly does not know it is Sunday.
Or that light is breaking out
All around the cutting-edge of the universe.

Leaves flutter in mid-summer breeze
Like a million green butterflies flapping in place.
Their quiet rustle interrupted
By short bursts of melodious bird song
And the steady beat of the cicadas.

All pauses in the low well of the wave
Poised in a moment of peace.

Still my mind sees hunger
Swollen empty bellies
Vacant eyes in a vortex of despair
Sad tribal conflicts staged on dry-cracked earth
Religious fanaticism and flag waving
Greed and overindulgence

Yes, this is a world of besotted minds
Abandoned bodies
Boxed horizons stacked upon an altar of fear

Slowly the world weathers into wormwood
With only this summer day
And a lone butterfly
To stand guard.

Look out!

Little Son of the Moon

Order, order, order
Causes few to earn
Their place beneath the moon.

Blind ruler, mutilator of individual law,
Wielder of shadows that shake us.

The holy select—Cervantes
Kafka, King or Kennedy
Who stood in the bright sun
Who slew the mighty absurd
The unconquerable and incomprehensible
The unquestioning and systematic—POWER!

Flags wave, candles burn, directives are issued.
Reflective and moon-like you few see clearly the many-faced enemy
Who lop the yellow limb of the rejuvenating monster.
Human nature, ultimate form of our ordered selves
That demands a desk-like obedience
With a mob-like violent and dumb will.

A mass hysteria of demands
Makes our footsteps in the shining night
Wayward and small impressions
Like a distant and briefly-known match brother
Blinking hopelessly good-bye in a daytime sky
Whispering
"Where are you father, my sons are in need?"

Go By Go By Go By

She cries now
Leaning against the front door
Five children just out the door
Off to the bus stop
This she can bear
But the cheating husband hurts deep
The abandonment wounds

What will the future bring
So many hungry mouths
Woman all on her own in the 1950's
An unadorned future
Less and less and lost
Looking for a miracle
That does not come

Do not tarry with your child's heart
But comfort her with your innocent love

We Salute You

War ok
Long as whole society wins.
Bad when few win.
Hunters should share in the kill

Your too fine-sifted advantage
makes me hate you over-indulged
"Bastards!"
Fat-fucker souls
bloated
on escalators ever moving up
while your hands throttle
the helpless rabbit necks,
but not eye-to-eye stare
then
people not scared
when you become President.

No!
They say
you know the ways of death
and its ever-present horror odor.
Like you smell me
down here.

You bastards must be dead
Like the digested stuff
of my entrails
on the pavement
when I think of you.

Like dirt on my *"blue suede shoes"*
All this bone dust falling from the sky

Too bad to energize your ineffectual being
I tell you you high-nosed low lifes
more criminal less guilt ridden than me
with your laurel wreaths
and bone-defined eyes.

Trump Change

There you stand
Tattered ribbons
Riding an old ass

Your adages sound wise
But do not ring true
What are you going to do about that windmill?

Quit you warped quixocity
Cast aside your negative ideals
See the round view

My vision does not jibe with yours
To me a closed system always loses
Your hate will not survive

There is fear in those who love you
Your tiny heart wants to grow
But your fright lies deep in rocky soil

Send yourself to the heavens before it is too late
My spirit waits to greet you
And hug your restrictive soul into a new horizon

A Foul Doom

The foul doom of our days
The dark whispering of suppression becomes a shout
Hate of other rises from a secret tsunami into a tidal wave

Evolution turns backwards to a time that never was
A raw violence that bleeding
Mob mentality, cowardice and ignorance the holy trinity
This thick air hurts
Difficult to breath this lethal smog

There are many angry voices on the lynching tree
Listen to the screams of the wind
This cacophony cannot be ignored
No matter your hateful drone

Waste Not Not

I always wished to be a war child, but was not.
No.
Conceived between a man too young to fight
        and a woman too, too young.
I am of the next wave—the Wasted Generation.
What a befuddled lot.
We idle idol worshipers
        bending toward the great earthly golden calf
        being carted to the landfill.
We fashion our redeemer, our grace the stuff of refuse.

You never know a moment: it is gone.
Good-bye strangers. Read me my tick-tock rights.

I love the rough seams that bind elegance.
The hidden cement behind appearance.
The restrained impulse of your moon rage.
The tender smile never shared.

To the glory of the impractical,
        let's put on lipstick and high gloss, hold hands and wish.

Father

Stars fall one by one
Takes an eternity to complete

Blue sky infinitesimal versus space
Darkness deeper than gravity
Black revenge against energies shine
A coming home to nothingness

Dark matter
Dark energy
So strong

What light on yonder sky-window breaks
Blue space shield of billions fate
Crustaceans piling on crustaceans
Footpaths for the passing

Impressions etched in sediment
Resting place of sentiments
Fade out on passions light
A dark joining in a living universe

And so the slow euthenization
Bright mind to distant sun
Slow onset of dim
Dance of forgetfulness and gone
Into the long night

Progress Isolation

The trains are faster
Sleek
The soulful wail gone
But still lonesome as the eighteenth century

Skyscrapers rise to the heavens
Sleek
Occupied ceiling to floor
But not connected

Cars line the highways in horizontal stacks
Sleek
Stretch to the horizon
Lost metal, plastic coffins to nowhere

Earth under tarmac
Species lost to construction
Sleek
Life under siege

Say goodbye!

War Loss

This long thought of dissolution must go
Yes your friend lies quiet
And the blast to your heart still burns

Your wandering continues into a friendless future
You step into a new aloneness

Stiff cliffs mark the boundaries
None can pass through those heights
There is only emptiness and missing

Your heart breaks over and over again
Silent cry soars like a bird over the horizon
Why are these empty spaces felt by so many?
Too many bruised deaths in this paradise

Out With It

I am going to stab passion
Oval canvas-fastened paintings
Painted passion
I am doing this because
I hate myself.

I hate myself because
I want to make myself real.
Because, more because,
I am afraid
And it is all in my head.
Or maybe isn't.

I do not know
If the knife will pierce
The canvas or glance
Off to me who I am stabbing anyway.

So,
Am I a man stabbing
Because that is the only way
To get out the man
Right now I am thinking.

There is the will to power.

I want to strike out.
I am desiring

The pressure breaking boiling
Kindling point of power will
and actions.

My fingers ache to be known.

The truth I want
And feed with my intellect
Is what I stab.

I stab into myself
To let out the oval scar.
The primal action.
I hate him.
Love him.
Me that is.

1988 St. Thomas Amen

Too much other out there.
Third world voodoo in the night,
Steel drum mumbo jumbo
Palm tree rhythm Caribbean wave beat
Sad face
Hardened, braced soul
Stiff lipped,
Rebellious balls of fist.

Stinging, covered, hurt
Run-down dirty streets
Forgotten many of six billion—
Hungry,
Earth dependent and sensitive souled
Shaped by combative other.

Driven to dreaming
Death waiting
Civilization trapped
Glorious spirits
Lying on the windowsill
With flickering last-moment eyes
Looking out
On an empty, dull parade.

The Furies Are on the Loose

The furies are loose
Killing the unexpected with drones in Yemen
Full of repression in Gaza
Holding on to favored status in Syria
Murdering in Nigeria and Somalia
Snuffing out hope with poverty in too many places to name
Inflicting suffering on pawns in the Ukraine
Alive in the prison cells of America for crimes of immigration and hopelessness
Rampaging through West Africa with Ebola and neglect
Killing the innocent of color in the U.S.
Selling lies and casting doubt on truth
Shooting freedom of speech with blazing guns
Poisoning the planet with unfettered growth and toxic waste
Throwing darkness on democracy and freedom all over the world
Driven by a ravenous vanity and greed
With insatiable appetite hurtling destruction.

HOPE

Hope—A Christmas Eve Reflection

Hope is not the conviction that something will turn out well, but the certainty that something makes sense regardless of the outcome—Vaclav Havel

Ragged cloak in cold of winter
Icy wind through a house of sticks
A sidewalk bed of concrete
A country spellbound by nonsense
Plague of hatred
Rudderless ship adrift in stormy seas
Children cast into the night because of who they love
Hunger hidden amidst a vision of plenty
Poisons of pollution cast into air with abandon
The earth subjugated to an ever-increasing demand
Gutted, gasping and aching
Cashed in like a lotto ticket
On this night there is much to anchor the soul
On this night there is a crying in the wind
On this night our spirits may be weighted
You may ask, "where is hope on this long night?"
Where is compassion and caring?
But do not be dazzled by the mantle of despair
Not while we have gratitude for so many blessings
Not while we have a vision of redemption
And the work of many restorative hands
Each to each sharing the weight
Aware of the millions of acts of love that light up a day
This is our hope—that we continue to build
That we march forward without certainty of success
That we carry in our hearts a more perfect vision
And act to make it happen

In this, the season of reflection, the season of gratitude
When winter chill blows and darkness has the edge
Let us remember we live in an expanding universe
And light bursts into nothingness in a constant act of creation
A stellar tide crashing on the shores of the universe
Let us remember that the story is ever unfolding
There are fair seas to the far suns
And a connecting love
Bones and stardust in the drift
Amid the caring space of our hearts
Tonight let us not make hope a ragged beggar
For hope is the last vestige of a survivor
Look!
There in the dawn
The rosy color of hope on the horizon
A gift for the taking to all humanity

And the Field Opens Wider

There's a field right in front of you
No direction
Nothing
A place to move and grow
No definition or definite
A place of possibility and fear
The nothingness that rises and becomes
And passes like a train whistle in the night

Your childhood, your friends
Your experiences, your meaning goes
Gone into the night air
The dewy humidity of your youth

Or something familiar that passes
Siren of allure and warning
Fleeting as a memory
That forever is forgotten
But speaks for this moment
Like a cry that says wait

Wake me, wake me
Do not forget me
As dawn rises for the last time
And night vibrates away
Blind and anguished

Howl, howl, howl
Distracted and mad
The shadow on the cave

Howls
Aware of its ignorance
Each philosopher king as pathetic as the last

Let it go in smoke
Let it go in illusion
Let it go because you must

Wave toward tomorrow
As it crashes against the delicate membrane of your life

Seeking
As the field opens wider

Mercy In Madness

There's a mercy in the madness
That helps me get along
There's a seamer in the sadness
With a haunting merry song
There's a murmur of your heartbeat
That I strain to, out of reach
There's a mercy in the madness
There's a mercy in the madness

A butterfly is sneezing
A storm begins to rise
A river it is flowing
To the sea through the countryside
There's a radio that is playing
All the jive is screaming round
In my head there is a motion
My spirit like a cloud

There's a mercy in the madness
That helps me get along
There's a seamer in the sadness
With a haunting merry song
There's a murmur of your heartbeat
That I strain to, out of reach
There's a mercy in the madness
There's a mercy in the madness

There's a screaming in my cereal
Bombs in my afternoon
There's a brother holding sister down

And sister doing the same
There's a tribal hatred going down
Like knives in a million sons
There's a mercy in the madness
Or I'd be on the run.

There's a mercy in the madness
That helps me get along
There's a seamer in the sadness
With a haunting merry song
There's a murmur of your heartbeat
That I strain to, out of reach
There's a mercy in the madness
There's a mercy in the madness

When the month hits late October
And the leaves begin to fall
The moon hits the horizon
Flowers blooming in the hall
It's then my spirit slips the haze
It's then I feel my person
At peace within the haunting maze

There's a mercy in the madness
That helps me get along
There's a seamer in the sadness
With a haunting merry song
There's a murmur of your heartbeat
That I strain to, out of reach
There's a mercy in the madness
There's a mercy in the madness

The Last Liberation

Last big bang banged
sandstorm of energy
rocketing around
limitless directions
like a motorcycle gang
on a mad rumble rampage
of clashing star chains
meteorite clubs
slicing switchblades
of cosmic heat
and exploding balls of noise
loud as the sum of all screams.

Magical high-speed chemical bombs
create bonded matter—
object
air, water
gravity—
existence!
Spinning orbits yet to stop.

The only moral imperative
aimless evolution.

I plug my feet into the ground
feel this rambling energy
raw speed in forced confinement.
Magnetic force:
energy in matter
matter in energy

captive atoms and cells
struggle always away.

Out
like an irresolute family
or an injured body
or the outside of an incomplete circle
or a man walking by

Our fetters
as necessary to existence
as skin. Our liberation as absolute
as stillness
as sure as
the last man
on the last night
with a lost lamp.

Our ultimate hope
to fulfill our destiny
racing light toward light
through space
with our brethren movements
all equal radiance
at the finish line.

The Deacon and the Wise Old Owl

Lazy with hunger
The deacon gets his sex with guilt
Alone in his room
The owl swoops in moonlight shadows

The owl jumps at the streetlamp
Thinks it's the moon
Stray dog wanders
Past dilapidated buildings

Wild owl in the window
A shriek of energy
A stunning vibration
Surprise flapping behind
Torn sheet shade

Everyone is asleep
Amid the alarm
Of this moment passing
The wise owl does not trust in accepted knowledge.

Why does the Deacon cry?
Why does your heart deny
This Energy that flows like a beacon
Beneath the owl's wings
On its way to heaven?

Nowhere to Land

A disordered flock
of birds
flies by
like an arrowed
errant
airborne
halo
searching among the millions
of us
for one who is redeemed.

Eureka

There the slim day runs sad
You sing a song to the mountains
Valley bursts with green

The river feeds your thirst
Winds its way to the horizon
While you search for gold

But it is muddish signs you find
And rocky value
Amid the quiet waving of the grass

A reflected light shines on your face
You talk to the far heavens
And blue night surrounds your thoughts

Dig deep into the earth for meaning
There is manganese in the sunset
Diaspora of your life
A golden alchemy of effort
Finds the rich vein of your heart

The Long Journey

I wait on high cliffs amid desert winds
And shifting sands
Looking out

Brilliant suns and bright moons rise and fall
The celestial burns like so many stellar bouquets
Sparkling in an infinite vastness
Stars like petals fall cooling into diamond clusters

Great shadows lurk
Sinewy and bending to accommodate any surface
Dark muscle of existence
Fast as fleeting

Light flickers ever tenuous
Thin flame amid so many good intentions
Yet bright flashes do emerge in the vast midnight expanse

Great thirst drives me from my haven
Dark earth and fertility are my quenching
Though wild beasts stalk the land
I follow the scent of my mind
Searching for the garden

The March Hare Runs

We miss you
All of you
We miss

You have gone before us
You breathed
You spoke

And touched
And sang
And felt
And longed
And hurt
And cried out
And felt alive
And danced

Were a part of each other
And the moment
And the stars felt right
And the moon was magic
And the winds caressed
And the deep ocean was vast and mysterious
And powerful

So profound was all
And you felt it fleeting
And you felt it cold

And you rejoiced in happiness
When certain moments went your way
And you suffered when hardship steamrolled
You or the ones you loved

And you felt it and knew it
As transient and gone

Still you hoped
Still you weighed good and bad
Happiness and sadness
Good fortune and bad
Still you ran
As one among the fertile course

And still you sought to express
The chaotic bustle
The objective other
The harsh march
Against the faint glow of the subjective
The brutal force of nature and time
Against the pale beauty
Of the beating heart

And yet you hope
For a magic gateway
Into a vibrating sea of joy

Tale of the Sad Oboe

Sad oboe sings my heart
Sparrow swoops against my blue skyline
Passing scenery blurry through the train window
Rows of apartments
Dilapidated houses
What is that rustling I hear?

Regal statues
Stone remnants
Kings of old
Unmoving stares
Frozen glory and vain pretense
Buried in the layered earth
Simple ghosts to whine in the wind

Brave hearts like grey photographs
Where is that swing set for my soul?
That exuberant buoyancy?
The freedom before the chiseled future?
The grave unwinding?

The bell tolls by the riverside
Reverberates past the shadows
And there
A saxophone of blue clanging
Background shambles of our lives

Even if the dance across the centuries is a stumble
You must not fall
But reside in a better vision
The children are counting on us

Solstice

Depart from this winter
Wait for me there in the month of May
I will to this frozen and rutted road

There is beauty in the starry bones poking through the skin of the sky
And excitement to this dangerous way

Do not miss me
Look among the colorful rags
Blooming like flowers in spring's abundance

Lost in the Heights

We thought there would be an apex
An ideal high up on the mountain
We climbed hard

Though stars guide us
Windmills fill our vision
A tangle swallows our heart
Deep web darkens our eyes
Sick sheep lie in fields

Soaring moon
Vivid sun

Dust falls from our hands
Our aim high
Our execution faulty
The scars no excuse
The stars there for us

Still we climb hard to the bitter end
Hope in these heights for a great flower to spring from our soul

When the World Falls Forward

When the world falls forward once again
Shatters our brains
Shakes us with fear

When, through serendipity,
Infinite moments collapse
Evolve into progress
Vast expanse of the world
Will once again shatter our brains.

Animals will walk proud in the wilds
The oceans will be our friends

Giant trees will radiate love
The air will circulate our cells
With joyous ascension

Plants will stretch themselves toward dominance
With the power of entropic assiduousness.

As always, we will tend toward mess
With hope of triumph

But when the world falls forward
It will lose its fecund sorrow of desires
And everyone will be free.

Holiday Invocation

We celebrate the holidays and our many blessings.

At this special time of year when winter chill blows and darkness has the edge, let us remember we live in an expanding universe and light bursts into nothingness in a constant act of creation.

From this expansive place, let us journey deep into ourselves to hear the still, small, authentic voice within each of us.

And, to know that from here to there, all is connected in a divine dance.

In the coming year, let us…
Live in awe of the great miracle of life.
Bring joy and love wherever we go and to whomever we meet.
Go forth with hope and accept whatever happens with equanimity.
Look for balance in our lives.
Try our best not to judge ourselves or each other with too harshly, but rather be accepting and always encourage towards the higher angels of our being.

May we be inspired with gratitude for the wondrous gifts that are ours.

May we be filled with resolve to share them with all who are in need.

May we hold precious one another,
And the world, which provides us with sustenance and beauty.

Inspire us to share the light as we delight in each other's company.

Amen and Blessed Be

FANCIFUL

August 14

It comes as a great surprise
just before dinner.
I remember the sunshine
yellow gold through the window
formed a halo over my head,
my mind heady with golden God.

I was suddenly assumed!
Taken!
Slapped in the face with unexpected sainthood.
Immaculate blessing shoved down my throat.

My substance departed,
my hot dog wasted,
Me, I'm miraculously wasted.
My God, why have you remembered me?

Grabbing at the table in desperation
I passed through the ceiling,
through the attic,
out the chimney,
into the heavenly clouds
to the ultimate home.

I pass out of history
a blessed miracle
listed as an unsolved
earthly disappearance.

The detective on my case, unfortunately, was a skeptic.

Moral of the Potato

Once
There was a giant
Potato
Strolling along the sidewalk.

A man
Picked up a rock
Threw it at him
Yelled, *"Get off the street you lousy potato!"*

All the people
Threw rocks at him
Every chance they got.

Well.
As things would have it,
This was no silent potato.
In fact, he was quite persuasive
And managed to convince
More than a few
Of his friends
To give up their miserous lot
To grow and become nomadic.

There were soon many potatoes.
Rather, they were well-educated
Verbal vegetables
That spread the awakening word
To many other inanimate races.

Soon
Carrots, broccoli
And all the vegetables
Walked.
Flowers opened their eyes
Even
Three musketeer bars roamed
With tête-à-tête swordplay.
All were animate.

A human was strolling
Along the sidewalk.
A potato
Picked up a rock
And decided it wasn't worth it.

Cosmic Ha Ha

There's a moment:
Glistens
Like a nonsense song
Forged in the smithy
Of a gigantic joke
Which reverberates
A cosmic solution
To the random movement
Of formed matter.

One moment:
A total summation
Of rampant energy
Like an out-of-control bus
In a Chinese night.

One moment:
Like a Styrofoam brick wall
Or a five-year-old
In Chinese fingers
That extend through time
With lethal Moe, Larry and Curly logic.

One moment:
That makes me want
To step on an ant
Or run around the house
Playing airplane.

I stand
With great pride
In line at the toll booth
To oblivion.

Restless

Grown tired of earthly nonsense
The moon grows wings
Takes flight
Soars past the Milky Way

Leaves a great emptiness
Of magic and deep reflection
A desertion of the highest
Silver slipper, Cheshire, half shine, full Man gone

Saturated by Saturn
Fully sated, but drunk with freedom
He dubbed himself Eagle Moon
And moved on
Free as a bird

What starry horizon does he seek?
What dark Olympus to find?
What star mountain of the gods?
What starry lover?

Eagle moon
We will miss your quiet observations
The balance of your light gravity
The many nights we took for granted

On the Plight of Halos

All those halos floating around
Looking for saints
Are as familiar as shadows.

I know halos.

They sometimes travel in groups
Disguised as cloud or mist or fog.
Most halos are homeless
Because they are not fooled
By a gentle caress
A passionate prayer of plea
Gentle demeanor
Or crumb tossing.

The life of a halo is not easy.
They have been hunted and marauded,
Impersonated and harpooned.
They have been betrayed.

Some—I suspect my Uncle Roland—
Have never even seen a halo.
Maybe a halo is best described
As a spiritual jellyfish doughnut.

Halos feed on good deeds and thoughts.
Although simple careless charity bores them.
They ignore the averted clink of the blind man's cup.
And flicker at the devoted committee man.

Halos are especially fond of Cubists
Or even Post Impressionists.

Halos, by nature, are judgmental.

Halos are better than purple hearts.

Dream Number One

I

They brought my brother in. Each
with a shotgun to his head.
Their names were Earl and Duke.
Evidently Brian
had roughed them up at the stadium
after they bumped him.
However, it seemed that didn't matter anymore.

II

My father went about his business.
Nobody but me noticed the man in the box
Under the sink
Singing:
There's a monkey in the sink
A monkey in the sink
A monkey in the sink
He noticed me listening and dulled his song
So I couldn't make out the words anymore.

III

Across the kitchen
the Bunsen burner was broken
At Earl's suggestion
I was sent to get the joker
which I found at the bottom of the third deck.
My father placed it under the burner.

It was fixed.
Everyone was friends.

I woke up laughing
        and on fire.

Having a Friend in High Places

Once, not long ago,
Lived a hybrid man
He had all the best qualities
And, what's better for everybody
He didn't know it.

So, while everybody
        Shone in his wit
        Nodded in his intelligence
        Walked in his grace
He grew despondent and finally shot himself.

When he died he grew tall and thin
Transparent and responsive.
"Ahhh, so the wind *is* ghost blowing around."

He whirled to all the best places.
Breezed into the *Gran Nacional* in Lucerne
Wafted into the *La Belle Epoch* in Tokyo
Typhooned through the South Pacific
And even spent the night on Forbidden Island.
He caressed the pages of the book of Kell in Dublin.
Became thick and heavy in the African jungles
Escorted killer bees through South America
Was caught in a test tube in Cape Cod
And made into rocket fuel.

He launched into space and was abandoned
Just outside of earth's atmosphere.
He marveled at Andromeda and the Milky Way

Cometed past Mars
Became bored by Pluto
Lost all hope on the galactic border
And dissipated soon afterwards.

He was last seen as a black hole
Last month in the *National Geographic*
The best magazine
The best guy I ever knew.

Got to Love Me

I am a fish lost in a cloud swimming in a blue sky
You cannot catch me

Soon I am a hook floating in an airy ocean
Almost caught a jet plane

There I go mist dragon
Wisping fire into a massive blue concave shield
St. George of the stars

Look at me
I am a cloud flower
Blooming white in a winter sky

Then comes the moonlight
As my deep red glow
Fades into your heart

Home on the Town

A house turns
Into a male person
And bows respectfully.

Tuxedoed
Wild eyes and hair
The elegance of the maestro.

His houseness snug
Hid in his hip pocket.
It exists delicately there
A hidden charisma.
A spirit deftly folded
As an embroidered kerchief.
A hidden resource of flair and savoir.

He stands Austrian erect
All resources centered
Full of steel, nails and hardwood.

Damp attic
May explain
His erratic actions
Out on the town for the night.

Sea of Madness

I notice Jonah floating there
Caught in a Styrofoam coffee cup.
I hold him.
He tells me he is going
To Merzda, the last city.

I'm hungry and dangle him
    On a string
        In the water.

He tempts me with cranberry sauce.
I hold out for a candle.
He talks of palm leaves and thunderstorms.
He promises vaguely
And hints of secret message.

I grow agitated as he tells
Of moss and growth.
Again he hints of someone,
A sort of cute daddy love I gather.
He nods and nods his moth-candy smile.

He yells of terror and fate
As I cast him back to the waters.

Seven Ways of Looking at Leonardo da Vinci's Front Teeth

I
High contrast there
Like a front door.

II
A reminder of you
Chinese splits
You not a meat eater.

III
All dolled up in your aspirations
Flapping paper wings

IV
Upside down
Looking like sutures
Paling your lower lip

V
As tiny dancers
In my sleep
Sharp and staccato
As I read my bible

VI
Leaning toward me
Always expectant
Unfulfilled in your Leonardo smile

VII

Old tombstones
On sandy you
Proven dead
At your request

Clumsy Tenderness

The werewolf within me is inflicted with kindness
My growls are an embarrassment

The wild and destructive within me
Is as threatening as summer rain

Where is my wolf libido?
Where my unrepressed and dangerous spirit?

Tame as a May shower
Soft and buoyant as Dogwood seeds
Floating on thin air

My threat is full of love
You will not find me in a dark alley
Or on a darkened bog

My claws are meant for loving

Flying Sunday to Wednesday Connection

From behind the chill, the tree
From beneath the ground
Where no waves are
I fall
A sentimental mixture without
Horns or parts
Here I am taught:
    To hate myself
    To hide things behind the backdoor
    To need your opinion
Here I have:
    Sweet melon on Sunday
    A tired mother
    A huge box in front of my face
    A wonder about what it's like
        To be
        Far away.
Here:
    The wind in the trees wins
    Minor battles against time.
    The forms Book and Song
    Are turned into radio chats and prick teases.
Here I:
    Get fucked every day
    Until I don't want it anymore.
    Look for a more sensitive instrument
    To direct myself.
    Want
        To be
        A happy old raisin

Sunning on the porch
Dreaming of some sweet
Wrinkle to conquer and know.
        To find friendship
With my arms wound tightly around me
My fingers crossed
Thinking flight.

Moral of the Piggy

He don't care
All day long
Snort snort snort
That piggy piggy piggy

See the murder of his friend
The quick chicken dance
Snort snort snort
Says piggy piggy piggy

Mrs. Schumacher

Everybody's going out and having fun
Except for Mrs. Schumacher
She's dead.
Died at 103.
Attributed her long life to spinsterhood.
She also claimed with a roar,
"I'm no Egyptian hunting cat."

Well…maybe so.
But her eyes definitely glowed in the dark.
And I would see scratch marks all around the W.C.
She herself attributed those scrapes
To a poltergeist gnome
That always hid behind the shower curtain.

This could possibly be true
As her students (She was a schoolteacher.)
Often felt a sharp pinch round the ankle
At even the merest thought of cheating.

When I would ask her if she regretted being childless,
She would always wink in a knowing way
Saying, *"DNA is AND spelled backwards."*

But what I loved most about her is the way
She would gaze trancelike out the window
And suddenly dart to and fro all round the living room.
I would laugh and laugh and say,
"If only you were 80 years younger."

And, she would say, *"Yes. When Schumachers were shoe makers."*
And pluck another whisker.

But you will have to excuse me now,
I hear a scratching at the door.

Gives me the Dickens!

Spirit and salt
Spittle and sputter
Words cannot utter

Cloud and blue sky
Mud in your eye
Cataract intact

Writhing and grieving
Hoping and healing
Soul unbelieving

Wind and way
Whistle and pray
Nothing will stay

Rain and pain
Muster inane
Nothing to gain

Heaven and earth
A life full of mirth
Never the twain shall meet

Perpetual light
Living in fright
Darkness and spite

Pairs to compare
Paradox and socks
Waves breaking hard on the rocks

Yin and Yang
Spaceships and Tang
Like Nietzsche said
All gods are dead!

The Great Escape

Without a doubt
The most prestigious
Of all people
Is the man
With the silver
Nickel-plated gun
That shoots toward
Untold areas
Of never to be
Believed sunshine
That I know
Will happen
If only someone
Would start it going
For a while
And then if nothing else
We could wander
Around the puddles
Of light.

Dance of the Cheshire

Night spirits rise from dark waters
Dancing light on foamy brine
Glowing midnight blue in the ocean air

Constellations sparkle in rhythm to their movements
Like starry messages transmitted from deeper space
Faded impressions of distant days
Lost love and long-gone ambitions

Free and unconcerned they move
No gravity to hold them
Like ocean spray they cavort
Movement by lithe movement
Conjuring a fluid passing
Skipping o'er the watery depths
These liberated transmissions of days spent
Smiling catlike in the firmament
With a questioning "Who are you?"

New Found Respect

My left foot…
I've always held
A special place
In
My
Heart
For my little toe.
Big, meaty big toe too
I've lavished attention.
Tallest toe and middle toe
I've loved, always loved.
Each has its own
Compelling attractions.
It's my fourth toe
Stoic
Stuck between baby and middle
Always ignored
The least nurtured
Of my digit children.
It's not fair!
How can I repay this
Eternal injury of neglect?
I cradle my fourth
In my spoiled fingers
Beg forgiveness.
What an admirable
Unpretentious little limb.
Always supportive
Dignified
Proud.

It's
The
Same
With
My
Right
Foot.

Origin of Death

"I don't know how I accumulated all this junk."

"You call that junk? That depends on your point of view."

"Well, at least it's junk when I have to cart it around like this."

"Depends on your point of view. Did you know about the space creatures?"

"Which?"

"The space creatures that are all around but you just can't see them. The ones behind the government."

"I didn't think anyone ran the government."

"Yea. Like who built that building? All these buildings?"

"You put grass in and out comes milk."

"Sour milk. Anyway, the supreme being created the seed. It's a miracle every time a flower grows. To build a computer as complex as the human brain, it would have to be as tall as the Empire State Building. And then it would be a clumsy brain at best. One cell is as complex as all life. See, man was created to live forever. But a space creature was put in charge by the supreme being. He has free will too. So, he disguised himself as a snake and told Eve she could live forever. She ate the fruit and God chased Eve and Adam into years of life. But, if they took care of themselves, they'd live forever. He just takes away the two-legged creatures that get in the way of

paradise on earth. The space creature perpetuates confusion with religions. But the supreme being proved to us we are all brothers and sisters because the joints of our toes are all the same. Right there he tells us we are all related."

"Geez, I didn't know that!"

The Vanity of Language

The next word
Comes from my mind
Without thought
Just write it down

And the next word
Until words do not come
Then stop

Or
Keep going
If more jumbles out

Or
If there is a case to be made
For this existence
To be meaningful
And not wasted or frittered away
With indulgence and fatted calf

Or
What if disaster lurks

Or worse
I desire comfort
But at least not extravagance

Just the pleasurable
To keep my thoughts
And speak with quiet energy

This would be a sign
Of a healthy mind
Not given to spout
The next word that pops.

War of the Absurd Hippophiles

Nineteenth-century horses on their way to war,
Hippophiles passively resisting
Are seized, put in stocks,
And released on their own recognizance.
Soldiers' swords are drawn with patriotic fanfare.
The horns sound and rapiers dance syncopated.
Slaughter sings a reaping tune.
Ladies drop their handkerchiefs and clap politely.

When tired, large draughts of vodka invigorate the swordsmen—
Remind them of who they are and for what their actions stand.
None caught cowardly stabbing in the back.
The media is there watching behind every tree
Looking for a Napoleonic warrior
With the intellectual underpinnings of a fine brandy.

The spectators sing rounds of "*woe-oh-woe-oh.*"
Dandies escort their ladies and place
Their chortled bets on bloodied warriors.
Oh to be first-born and landed—
No need for the thrust and parry of the swordsman.
A sire, a cocksman with culture to be
That makes one free to sniff the snuff
With an elegant turn of the head just so.

The horses dance to Strauss waltzes
As they plunge into the fray.
Fickle fate murders committed fidelity on both sides.
Survivors retire for fine wine and meaty mutton.
Wounds are swooned over.

Even in war people act like characters casted
In a well-directed play whose nihilist meaning
Never really becomes clear until you're
Staring at a white cloud and a strange yellow sun
And the breeze washes your spirit into the blue sky.

But the absurd hippophiles will be there to fight another day.

Outlook

It is not seven o'clock and time to get up but it may as well be. I am lying in bed and someone is knocking at the door. The room sharp, a Cezanne or Monet. I drift in the room past the dresser that folds toward me in embrace. The lamp post bows, framed wide angle. My saxophone soft and pliable as a caterpillar rests in its velvet cocoon. This carpet bustles, anxious as a telephone. The pair of plaid pants I had expected, quiver impatiently through the keyhole.

We drink coffee. He reads the local newspaper, *The Munich Sensation.* There's a naked body on the first page. The headline is, "Midget Put Up To…" but he turns the page before I can finish. I ask him to turn back, but he doesn't hear me. He says my eyes look like rusty metal vaginas. I tell him he should read another newspaper.

The small room surrounds like a corset. I want to circle round him and squeeze him, putty into a ball. I want to stretch him taut, hang him out the window, and crawl down the street.

He says some local terrorists have issued a statement asking for a two-hour moratorium. "Let us have our dignified deaths and vague moments of touch," was their plea. He says a recent survey concluded that even ugly people of one race can win handsome lovers from another. I wanted to look out the window, but felt his eyes sneaking up on me every time I did. Then everything went dusty.

Stinker and Blinker

I am sad
Or maybe mad
Perhaps even glad

Do not think
Try not to stink
Don't even blink

Binary computer finery
Drinks in a winery
Canary in the minery

Perspicuity
So damn rickety
Plain old chicanery

Sweat like a pig
Out of your wig
Like the beatniks you dig

What does it mean
This life like a dream
Row down the stream

Stars in the sky
Don't even ask why
We're all gonna die

The Tale of the Concerned Pig

An old actor
grows deeply bitter
like the forgotten shoe
of my dead father.

The worn skin of King Lear
borne in the air
a vibrant tragedy
to be contemplated from an armchair.

The wrinkling of crisp paper.
The clapping of hands.
I hear their vibrations
in our embrace…

In our patriotic songs,
in our call-girl desires,
in the random scratchings on rock,
in the cover coming off our bones.

The bell tolls heavy three times
and everybody laughs.
Your final lines rage
resonate with unnoticed spittle.

Five billion chairs
for five billion kings.
No gold for crowns,
no wood for chairs.

No body for your spirit
I pause my snort snort
in a moment of tender concern.

Good-bye snort snort.

Tongue in Cheek Lover

Part French lover
Part Swordsman.

Amore. Amore.
Pass me red wine
From your red lips.
Our kisses spread
Wine out wet,
Redden our bellies.

Kiss our back thigh
Our inner thigh.
Share our intimacy
With distant friends, strangers
And the so well known
As to be almost unseen.

Let the bird in us float
Wings spread
Windy cool breeze.

Trace our shore downstream
Our beak slanted.
That part of us takes up
With a pack of ducks
Heads south to the sea.

Coo Coo World

Spring snow
The robin sings
Coo coo coo coo
He is so right.

HOMAGE

Bland Ole James Joyce

Swigger-cane weave down the street,
sniggler for Lifey
flow gently unto me.

Hands across the river,
message in yellow leaves.
Turn over rare thoughts.
Smother me with the obscure.
Profound me with the particular.
Blath me with rich new language.
Blaster me with new meanings.
Forge sentiment in my half-cockled cells.
Crackle me with Kant can't you you
ham rent with puns. You

gross indiginer of riddled labyrinth.
Earth occupies your message.
Dreams form the stubble of your face.
Swagger me with the rhythms of your languish
like magic brooms out on the town all night.
Retremble me with kissin' words.
Write trouble meanings.

A couple of dimes and a tink...
I tink there must be a link,
but I don't know what it is.

Do you James?

Scott-free

I hold my sides,
Think about heroes.
I want to cradle
All the heroes. Take
Their pain away.
Give them that long
Cry of relief. Restore
Their bodies to youth,
Their ideals to their hearts.
Give them a quiet room,
Fulfill all their desires:
    Warm baths
    Sleepy brother buddy conversation
    Good fucks
For all the heroes.

Let them have full brave flight,
Many places to go and many times.
Let them out of sick beds full
Of damp urine and belly torture.
Let them go their ways victorious.

William Burroughs Cut-up

It wasn't serious at first.
This sort of random craving for images.
I'd read in a newspaper something that reminded me of or had some relationship to something.
And then I'd cut it out.

I'd be walking down the street and suddenly see a scene.
I'd photograph it and put it in a scrapbook.
Association blocks rather than words.

When you start thinking in images you're well on your way.
Cutups establish new connections between images and one's range of vision consequently expands.

I was sitting in a lunchroom in New York having doughnuts and coffee.
I was thinking one *does* feel a little boxed in New York.
I look out the window and there was a great big Yale truck.

That's a cutup, a juxtaposition of what's happening outside and what you're thinking.

No, at first it was no more serious than vague theory and thought process expansion.
But it got worse.
It became a preoccupation.
I had huge files of picture and script I'd carry everywhere.
I took to traveling by train or ship to hold the bulk of this well-ordered collage.

I jotted down everything. Then from notebook to tape recorder.
Everything noted.
What seen at time of thought.
What book on lap.
Who next to me.
Where I was in motion and geography.
The perfume or flower.
My preoccupation.
All.

Personalities developed and were named. Green Bpu, Izzy the Push, Green Tong, Sammy the Butcher, Willie the Fink, Dr. Benway.

What does this force; and insatiable appetite for word and image; propose to do with such a tremendous amount of backlog.
What to do with this giant festoon of resource.

The hope lies in the development of non-body experience and eventually getting away from the body itself, away from the three-dimensional coordinates and concomitant animal reactions of fear and flight, which lead inevitably to tribal feuds, dissension and psychic schizophrenia.

The main thing though, is for me and us to get away from the All-American Pepsi-Cola cowboy way of thinking.

Cut!

An Unworthy Quixote

Empty bushes gloss the landscape
Like the limp lives of third world countries.
Rosinate, my dreamy horse,
I ride you into the horizon of my ideals.
Brush away the dust of my dust
I believe in all that grand-maker, bru-ha-ha nonsense.
Especially when I drink vodka and laugh.
A great rhythm vibrates my ash-targeted bones.
So divine a steak urges transmigration into animal flesh.
God created animals for man's use without promise of eternity.
This steak makes me live for today
With my nervy urges and pleasures of simple sensitive skin.
My purple beliefs are regal stupid hearts.
Better to believe in red meaty reality.
An errant night fulfills my ideal pleasure.
Bless me with a case of wine and a lovesick lover.
Make me sane with your warm cuddlings.
Desires, lead me to a happy future
And a dreamy horse
And a defenseless windmill.
I heard You once but burnt bushes are empty.
My small horse seems so tiny on these busy roads.
Give me bread to eat you bastards!
Save some for me you shits!
My shape, caught in a proud moment,
Imagines dignity in my pursuits.
I touch the ground
And my head hits the sky.

Absurd as Mambrino's Helmet
I am inept to serve others.
Yet my love outlives my hate in a half-full glass.
Amen if you please.

Poepuns

Tradition:
Snows
in the
past passive as
old shoes.

Low. All
but unseen.
Here,
a weak
pounding
from the
past an
itch.

Will
yums me tummy
a punished
object.

Care
O
Care
O
Care
O
ache.
Care
O
ache.

My father
died of
gin an
iceberg
in
Gins
berg.

Tradition:
Snows
in the
past passive as
old shoes, a slow
steady fan,
a soft breeze
on my cheek.

Shine On

Where the sun departs the horizon
Where my heart falls to earth
Where my way collides with gravity
Is the loss your passing brings

Where your vision lit the future
Where your passing brightened so many
Where your light guided the path

This is where I stand
Thinking of you
In all your illumination

John Lennon Dreaming

Some word gets to the heart of crazy.
Blazing sun 1967
Makes me think of you.

Searching, searching yellow matter you.
Tell me your dream
Over and over again.
Different clothes
Nice rhythms
Screaming dream and imagine and laughs.

Your mother
Her finger through her empty glasses
You, in a constant state of stranded.
Bridgette Bardot your perfect animal object.

You
Always try to wrap
Yourself in circles
And see your way out.

You meant so much to me—
Sound waves
Words

Your life a photography of events
Sent with an uncomfortable itch of body.
Taken away.

I miss you.
Good luck.

The Streets of Altamont

Holy Christ! Dead at 38—
And of pneumonia as predicted
By purse-lipped Eliza,
All caused by your slumped walk.

Why in comparison to your output
A train whistle screams a long time—
Perhaps with near the feeling
Though without the detail.

Ben, the older brother, led the way.
A stone, a leaf seem random.
Don't you know you were meant to be?
You a fast growing tree of genius, rustling

And far-flung leaves, so many fecund.
Why my living grandfather was born before you.
I wish to God we were arm in arm
Like two angels well realized.

Limb of limb and stone free
Blessed with that magical language
That bridges the void between
Our awakenings, our longings, our deaths.

You, A Delicate Kafka

Make your way into the great mists of morning
What images float in the diaphanous ethers
These are but the possibilities of your mind
As you search for a clear road forward

There are cobbled streets in Prague
An abusive past
The helpless wriggling of the observed insect

You in your lonely room
Betrayed by Father
Never peace to be found
By all, all around

The door will never open to your knocking
It is mystery that does not dissipate into morning dawn
That closes heavy on your heart
The riddle that can never be solved
Even in your best imaginings
And the only door you can open!

Philip Hoffman Seymour Gone

His addiction the same as mine
Love of life with an anxiety that will not yield
Clutched in a jangle of nerves that cannot be soothed
Except in an addiction
That quiets the scream

When I close my eyes I hear the high scream of my nerves
Feel sympathy for your needled death
And sorrow for the legacy loss
That must be borne by those you left behind

I breathe deep in this passing of time
And say yes to a peace in my heart
That always hovers just beyond
Coaxed close by the seduction of your talent
Your many performances that said, "Hold on."

Of Jerzy Kosinski

Your mind a cruel morality.
A vehicle of justice when need be.
You, like a transmitter, uninvolved.

Your friend, a Russian.
A world-renowned fencer.
He did not defect,
But spoke of it in New York City.
When he returned to Russia,
They broke his hands.

They had bugged his room
As you found out.
You coaxed the perpetrator,
Played on his greed,
Into a bathhouse.
Tied his neck, arms and feet
Bow-shaped together.
Buggered him with a sword.
Left him dead.

This a blind date you abandoned
To a cell pegged away and forgotten.

Later, you laughed,
When I told you
Of the American in Russia
Who,
Convinced his room was bugged,
Spent his first night searching it.

He noticed a soft spot on the floor.
Pulling back the carpet
Revealed a small trap door.
He opened it.

Surely a microphone.
He took to unscrewing
The egg shape.
Turn by turn
His righteous anger built.

There was a huge crash below
As the chandelier hit the floor.

LIFE

Shaman Master

I am owl
Silent
Solitary
Vigilant watcher
Living stealth
Swooping moonlight

I am bison
Sinew and muscle
Tornadoes of breath
Roaming power
Locomotive of flesh
Stampede of spirit

I am coyote
Howling madness into a midnight moon
Blues singer of existence
Scavenger of sustenance
Moon lover and star gazer

I am lizard
Long of ages
Survivor of passing
Slow heartbeat
Reptilian responder
Slow of movement
Quick to action

I am raven
Winged messenger of prophecy and insight
Harbinger of death
Omen of passing

I am strong in wound and way
Vigorous hunter
Dangerous and daunting
Strong antidote

I stand in the wild forest
Amid the howling roar
And soar on high in stormy winds
Kin to moonlight and shadowed ways

Brave too beneath the stark sun
And barren lands
All things are in me
And I in them

This is my kingdom
These are my visions

Tribal Beasts

When sun exists it shines
Nature made it that way
Water is wet and earth dirt
What nature we?

Two legged and ambulant
Makers of thoughts and things
Hunters and killers
Parasites of the earth
Consumers and fear filled
Lovers and leavers
Self involved and kind
Compassionate and confused
Worried and harried
Reachers for the stars.

Sailors and navigators
Discoverers and dancers
Dreamers and meditators and grand transgressors
Insane worshipers and believers of superstition
Rationalistic and uncaring
Blind to everyone but ourselves
Shadows
Illusionists
Sure when we are wrong
And wrong when we are sure
Breathers and polluters
Courageous and foolish
Pawns.

Pale imitation of our true selves
And greater than our capabilities
Wanting and desirous
Questioning
Aware of the mystery and willing to imagine
Any insanity to explain it.
We take our very best impulses
And turn them to evil
Powerless and destructive
Doubters, believers
We burn with a dull light
A complex gravity
A grave confusion
A great halo of misguided intentions
Gangs of sorry intent reaching for the stars.

Caught Here

That infinite place between you and me.
The fluid interchange
Of subjective and objective:
    A breezeway of delight and horror
    Where the impossible meets physics,
    Where murder meets blood.
    Where love encounters skin.
    Where a bubble of imaginary identity
    Meets a mad knife of uncontrollable action.

An out-of-control train bursts through my cells.
Sex and death dance in my being
With the innocence of a cheap hotel.

An off-course outside,
The brick and mortar of my limitations,
Guides my spirit;
Rules the realm of the sublime.

The objective flag flies
Hoisted at the pinnacle of my mountain
Like an endless list of restraints
Or a thousand million movies
Of adventure and danger,
Love and entanglement.
My substance confused with seas
Of needless information and movement.

Your times of war
And spirits of flight,
Of bodies caged,
Minds dreaming of better times.

I cry over the weight of our hearts,
I hold hands with your voice
Projected from my incomplete knowing of you.
Your useless actions beat in my ears.
The rampage of your darkness scares me.
Immobilizes me.
The call of your love opens my eyes.
The fear of your loss,
Tied to my existence,
Animates my nature.
Waste,
The imperative of your spirit,
Seeks to reign in my intelligence.

I imagine my mind noble.
My song in the darkness
Beckons my spirit up
Against my nature,
Against gravity and the rule of your law
Which, like a voice from the heavens,
I bow to in fervent angelic conversation.

Come To Me Sweet Fantasy

Come to me my sweet fantasy.
On a bus of liberation
Sweet dreams come true each mile.
Dancing New Year's Day
With all windows open.
Going 70.
Someone you trust driving
Up and down beautiful mountains.
The road twists and baffles
But not enough to effect
Our direction or safety.
I express my amazement
To everyone's amazement.
Not just in words,
But in every motion of my body
And throughout points of existence.
Best of all, my cells sing love.

What rejoicing we all share—
Guns go limp
Ill humors fall earthbound
Swallowed, burned and released
In liberating form.
How fortunate your dream positive
And I can look on the pink pulsing
Beneath my thumbnail with pleasure and hope.

Unfortunately,
I see you smokey spirits
In the distance

And your hell scares me
Like the garbage dinners
I am afraid of in my future
Of little faith.

Hymn of the Cherubim

Liberation through suffering
Body prone
Spirit buoyant, sitting up,
Ready to fly.

Eyes already rolled up.
Brain high contrast
Static and noise.
Worry already creeping
Down into the cold
Of your toes.

Fear receding into icy
Transparent skin.
The clouds give up their shape
To the mystery informing.

The secret stored in your lips
Released but dies quiet
Lost before being uttered.

One frantic hand still grasps
For something to hold onto,
Like a passenger in an airplane
That falters in the sky.

Tiredness needles its way
Through skin to air.
A heavy weight falls earthward.
Your senses give way

To a more direct, uninterpreted communication.
Hymns rise around.
You wake, gather your
Angel sisters
And head for the stars.

Looking for Night Vision

There is only one way to go into the woods
Wild in spirit
Wide eyed
No thought of being lost
Just deep into the dark

There is no path
Just bramble and thorn
Root and bark
Fallen
Thick ways through the forest

The noon sky is in deep gloom
High over the swaying trees
But no help to your navigation

Perhaps the stars will shine through
And amid this darkness
You will find a way through

Another Party

The fans spin
As language circles
Like a dissipated star system
Bereft of gravitational attraction

Long fingers grasp at diminutive cigarettes
Their lives up in smoke

Thin our lives
Few notice
None last

Deceptive to ourselves
We clamor
In black leather
And short skirts

In meaningful stares
And disinterested looks
In private, intimate conversations

That glow in the stiff breeze
Of passing

Like that moment you realize
You are gone
And they are not.

Memory Project

It was before birth
We were all together:
my three brothers, my sister, my mother, father and me.
We were not children nor adults.
Time lay around us in warm blankets.
We did not have vision or space.
There was no judgement
good, evil, joy, sorrow, important or not.
There were no lonely airplanes.
There was no movement.
There was not weariness.
We were not in rows.
There was no aggression.
Purpose did not exist.
I do not know if we needed each other or not.
There were other places where things were different.

Places with people.
And people believe in things.
They believe in maps and future,
Recall and movement.
The movement was not heard.
Time runs over them in boulders
they catch in envelopes and file.
There is diversion and influence,
an idea of sense.
There is waiting and blunder,
capsules and derivatives.
There are walls,
definitions, diversions, misconceptions.

There is over there,
high, low, near, far.

It is my turn. There is me.
There are names and others.

At the age of two we moved from a house on Manhattan Street to our home at 445 Wilshire Avenue. I thought we had moved because of the ghosts that had tremored their wispy racket through the house at night. It had not bothered me as it had blended quite well with the locomotive howl, the airplane whir and the silent presence of the oil drum round back. Besides, we got on together. But I believe it bothered my parents, and so we moved.

Then I remember the stare. Her eyes wide and unseeing in the calm of Sunday, Sky King and coffee comics. I remember the due that had been paid and embodied in the stare unseeing, the eyes bugged out dry, cracked highway eyes, forgotten ribbons, no prize.

I remember the watchful waiting of the learning of the clock mechanism till the playtime day could possibly begin. I remember mud puddles, their bottomless movies to be stepped into, walked across and *really* surprised when my foot reemerged undigested.

And there was Halloween and October. The long purpled fingernails and probable vulture teeth of the popcorn-anima-Merlin across and beyond the first tar shadow.

And I remember restless wanderings, vague imaginings. Eating a nut completely out of touch. Broken faces baked in clay.

There is a house.
It's on fire.
There is a woman inside.
She has always believed and trusted,

counted on otherness.
They carry her outside.
There is a crowd.
There is not a crowd.

There is tenderness.
We are not tender.

There is an energy out there.
The opening of a car door.
The movement of head and hand.
The oscillating knee.
The furtive movement of flashlight.
And dark.

There is an idea of separation:
that chair, this couch,
plant, snail, bat and grapevine.
Maypoles, sandlots, Tahiti, Japan,
Alvin, Mr. McGoo and the danger of scissors.
Birthday-to-birthday feelings of accomplishment.
Men defined only by the space around them.
Gun shots in dawn.
Deer heads and front yards.
Mice in the kitchen, and traps.
There are tantrums and the comfort of warm dryer.
There is static electricity,
pants clinging to socks,
screaming snakes upstairs.
Alligators around the bed,
mountains on top.
There is Wild Bill, Bat Masterson.
The hardness of good,
the hope for a test.
There is trying to trick God,

faking left, going right—
one hundred black blankets and still no place to hide.
There is the comfort of shadow,
bike carnivals and kids down the street.
A pocket full of keys,
forgetfulness and comfort,
loss, comfort,
rest.
Tiny flashlights of warning unheeded in their sidewalk homes…
and gifts.

Thousand Island Mental

SOS to the thousands of my mind
yearning to rejoice
in their unlimited dimensionality.
My mental islands communicate
across gaping chasms blind-walking
a frayed tightrope backwards.

Many times must resort to two
tin cans, some sting and scream
loud shouts of simple need or simply nonsense.
Too upright to talk complex
I speak a thousand smoke signals
that dissipate into simple moods.

My mind curls in upon itself
a floating fist, tight as an ice cube,
among the billions of fists
barely ambulant, using a walker
or propelled along
on some technological wheelchair:

Video. Film. Computer. Expensive restaurants.
Wide-bodied jets. Seven countries, four days.
Electric guitar, transcendent sound blazing lightening ego.
Compact discs of *Ave Maria* digitally
reproduced from the original, primordial
angelic choir—first chorus of God.

My thoughts coded in screeching
out of tune violin string

swept by an eternal bow.
This aggravating brain chorus blinks
SOS behind my eyes. These neuron
messages impose themselves on my short circuits
plumbing me into my full depths where
I listen without a muse.

However, fortunately, occasionally, I pull out a plum.

Arthur's Lament

Mine is the moment the sword is drawn
Damocles hangs in the balance
The vulnerable throat drinks Sherry all alone

The risks are high for each of us
Moment by moment
Merlin, where is your magic?

There is triumph in my eyes
A belief in round justice
A democratic sharing of ideas will lead the way

But Lancelot cannot bury his compassion
And how much worse the sputtering narcissist

So the grail is never found
My sword goes powerless against a wave of dumb fear

These ways lead towards destruction
And the lost way

Yet vulnerable throats recoil to the streets
Bolstered by a leathery strength

Of Matter and Nonsense

Like breath, caring fills my void
Round and feminine
What is this place where lives
Disappear behind doors?
Where rules seem arbitrary
As the movement of stardust?

Hitler, Stalin, Caesar, Akhenaton
Many others ruled to their own end—millions lose!
How many die for the petty
Comfort of others?
O Socrates, does intellect lead to order?
Aristotle, do we seek happiness
When every hood act risks eventual bad end?
Should we muster our might to judge intention?

The scattered impulses of billions
Fly like aimless hailstones.
Shall we gather meager protection?
Or seek the inevitable good-bye of fate?
Or hoop our bodies around the needier?

Do our monkey bodies generate our spirit?
Or will we go our separate ways
Each to join in a more essential process
Body to earth, spirit free to spirit?

Put on your mask and show me your true face.
Problems, nihilism, I consider my self
And some part of me says you.

One hand grasps the other like strangers
Whose energy caps the blue sky
Imbues wheat with love or hate.

Dumb clay cakes my soul.
Trees hang from the earth
And point toward the sky.
Most efficient senses
Ignorant of heaven
Blunt instruments of survival
My spirit points north
Toward evergreen skies.

Let others thrash.
My thoughts float like a balloon
Heavenly missile heading skywards
Destined to land on some distant shore
Broken and full of pride
Amid the wastebasket of history.

Bird-brained Starlight

This bird on the wing sings soprano
Clipped
Rigged like a cliched two-bit election.
Nothing inspiring here
No new horizons
No flayling, liberated guitar solos
No energy turned electric flight
No no no no no

Until like finished rock sculptures
Defined beyond subtlety
I heave unimaginative yawns to the stars
Who respond in kind
With sleepy stories of domination
By black restlessness
And the urge to exchange light.

On Being Different

I
Isn't it scary
To be black
In a white neighborhood?
An anonymous angst
On the stride of good?
Dead weight to be fleeced?

I try to prove myself
To the stars.
I do not believe
They listen
To my lengthy arguments
I may as well be talking to a rock.

Above all the vast yearnings
High above aspiration
I ride the wind of discourse
To the sky of eternal essence.
I dance
A pagan dance
Of freedom, murder
And abstract calculation.
I anger animal spirits
With my perfected human form.

II
The boy always cries
Fish flow in his tears.
Ships sail. Men drown.

Myths grow.
All you my mothers and fathers
Grow rich on my smile.
I pound on cloud.
Rebel at blue sky
With back to sun
Hands tied
Fingers crossed.

Nauseating noise of planet
Gathers in spring waves.
Ancient collective monsters
Scream of most fearful superstition
The sad stories of the animal.

I kiss your ass and forget.

III
Gazelles, giraffes, elephants and lions—
All wild beasts rest.
The demons of Germany rest.
The mythic Indian deities sleep.
Proteus rests in forms of subconscious change.
The Neanderthal has seen his nights under the moon—
Uttered his desires.
There's a darkness around the vegetable world of the East.
Heroism too rests.
Cowards rattle their bones in involuntary rhythms.
You've already stared at the door for hours
Outside
While laughter and conversation flowed inside.
Your hands have trembled with excitement
At the thought of two hands alone.

IV
We touch
Through a billion transient hands
A billion shared impulses
Trillions of whispering ideas.
Survival is a deadening itch.
Drunk with the music of the stars,
Kin of monkeys,
God flutters in our breast.
Singing angels suffering.
We, suffering from gravity,
Strain to move mountains.
We act in accordance with our being.
Grasp at miracles.

Liberating humor of the tomb,
Comfort me in my hour of need.
Gracious purveyor of my breath,
My million dreams of you
Are refuge from the haunt.
Liberated from the shrinking
Limit of my life,
Limber toward time,
Bending to your will,
I share myself with existence.
Point myself toward the stars.

V
An eternity of folly under the revolving sun:
Neurotic Don Quixotes,
The hunter after the whale,
The drama of self.
What conscience urges folly?
Creates meaning?
Dreams?

Transcends?
What dreamer of self creates crosses?
Demands a kingdom to die in?
A throne to sit on?
Oh to rule!
To rule for a moment on a passing wave beneath the sun.

VI
Fortune burns red.
Water filled with gas.
Loud sounds in the hallway.
Noise through the walls.
Somewhere
A cat lurks,
Gun in hand,
Chewing a cigar.
My mind exists in the sky.
The details of my senses hardly matter.
Breaks squeak.
The sun sets again.
Medaled soldiers, now old,
Meet to remember.
They dance drunk
Wondering what happened.
My message is a simple, helpless one.

VII
I paint myself in time
A thousand colors of joy
A million unknown delights
A million voices calling for completion.
One life, ten million dreams:
        Musician, lover, hanged man
        Hungry midget, saint, artist

Tortured dancer, priest, drunkard
South American…
Each has its own attractions.
Drowned in sensation,
I rise with the dignity
Of an old hotel room
To take my place in the heavens
My body released into an eternity of action.

Business Lunch

They gather to fill themselves
With meats and breads,
fat and flesh,
fish and fowls,
sweets and drinks.
Round bellies grovel
Like gangs of rabid bears on the loose.
Digestive juices attack the defenseless,
already dead animal and plant.
There's no end to our parasitic abuse.
A boulder-sized belly ball,
As huge as Rhode Island,
A crushing behemoth,
A leviathan of blubber,
Smashes its way through my imagination,
Ruining my appetite.

The only thing worse,
The fake and scheming conversation
Disgorging from trembling chins and spotted ties.
Voices murmur like an idiotic jazz
Of pathetic and vain pursuits
Accompanied by silverware clinks,
Emphatic and sincere gestures.
The lights are dim, thank god.

Hardwood and stain glass,
Imitation 19th-century paintings
Show a life as grotesque, if less crowded.
The immigrant poor wait the tables
And ignore their globulous patrons.

Wild Time

Time runs like a pony
Heading west like the wind
As they say.

Whoosh, there it goes
Running away fast now
Whistling with anxiety
Worry, worry, worry goes the world.

Take deep breaths
Hang on to a rock
While the wild winds of time howl.

Pack of dogs is time
Yipping and ripping at existence
Turn your energy quiet
After a while.

Goes still.
And you don't know where
Out for a spin I guess.

Precious Jewel

Tender hearts of youth
Like gossamer glass
Ill prepared for the long journey
But strong of purpose

Deep spaces and mysterious darkness
Windows, bright lights and moving shadows
Non-descript figures shuffling in fog and night without direction
Diaphanous and murky past

So much loss in my mind

Is the future a wild and roaring lion
Or a sweet embrace?

We have come a long way with delicate preserve
This precious object, perhaps a heart-shaped locket
Or a necklace dangling a wounded bird

Sugar Mountain

It was so beautiful
Pure snow and an LSD high
Wind whirling my molecules
In a cold invigorating flight
On this wild and exhilarating night

This is "Sugar Mountain"
This that moment in the sun
When the universe aligns
When 15 years old is rapture

Do not bother me with your loss
Do not tell me of the myriad cuts that drain and
Wobble your way

My fragile and innocent spirit lifts
Makes angel wings in the sky
Soars over a domain of sweet abundance
Fully alive in a starry sky that says yes!

Cruel Invention

Like the sadness of a small TV screen
    pulled from my seat on this 747

Or lament with heavy and sad horns

Your music consists of cold mechanics
    and impersonal circuits.

Efficient and perfect and non-human
    "You Bastard!"

You don't even react to my beating.

No bleeding and screams from you.

Blind subservience and nothing
    else matters.

I long extensively to turn you into a tree
    or some living thing who will regret
    loss of animation.

You are the closest thing to "high culture"--
    a business atmosphere with no sense of finite.

Don't you regret?

Feel something or die.

I wish I could kiss your antithesis,
    like an old acquaintance who once defended
    me in spite of my powerlessness.

All I know is you are something
    that scares me
    and I run into you more and more.

Leave my kids alone you bastard.

"Life is <u>not</u> a highway!" It's an embrace.

It Calls Outside and Feels Like Me There

I can hear it happening. My voice calling
But not so far away. Near
Like just out the window
Or on the other side of the door
Or at night from under my bed.

Sometimes I hear it in wine bottles.
Or it talks to me through smoke.
What sometimes happens
Though is that
I hear it
From under my nails. I
Clip, bite, tear to hear it better. To
Get closer. Underneath the nails
And the skin. Inside and into my blood
And small I get. Hard to notice. But still
I cannot sneak onto it. I cannot find it.
Until next thing I know
I am lying in bed
And the voice is coming from the walls
And people ask me who am I talking to
They say it's nonsense
They say,
"Calm down, calm down. You will over exert yourself."
But I am fine. They are the ones.

Well get out!
You don't have to listen.
In fact you scare it away.
You blur it.
But I don't want to go to sleep.

I don't want to go to sleep.
I don't
Want
To
Go
To
Sllleeeepppp...

In Gratitude Awakened

Wait, the world grows old.
The ancient gods are tired.
Weary from overwork—
The seas restless stirring
The green grass browning in a stark sun
Flowers stripped of their nectar.
A sleepy fog grows like a misty future.
One without hope and the gods asleep.

Lost to new and false gods.
Distinct brands saccharine and sweet.
Full of heaven and hell fire.
Bereft of life force and body and sensation.
Deniers of the animal.

Where is pagan animation?
Appreciation for moments in the sun
So fleeting, so besotting, so alive
Invigorating as they pass into ether
Full of a profound but fleeting meaning.

Let us find our courage, recognize our transience.
Let us join the ancient gods
Stirring in the valley.
Lift them to the mountain.
Raise them in the sun.
Let them dream of new pastures
And a green tomorrow just springing into existence
To wake the senses in liberation
And find joy in the reality of this ever-going world.

Reflections in Spring Snow

Spring snow falls on the mountaintop
Last invigorating chill of the season
Wakes you.

Moonlight infused by fog floats in the night
The magic of darkness resonates with the lost moments of your life.
There in the mists you see your moments in the sun.

So many ways and friends and moments
Strewn across the landscape of your life
Images projected by the light of a smokey strobe candle.

Sweet vibrations of love and lovers
Gone to their own swift paths
Their sweet touch emerges in the misty glow of early spring
Snow wafting like a life-giving manna
That energizes for the road ahead.

Turn your head towards the future
Leave your clinging loss where it belongs
In the surging waters of spring
Roaring down the mountain
Into a new tomorrow.

Sorrow's Whimsy Likely Flows

And so another Christmas passed
Winter solstice grows deep dark
Spouts growing sunshine
Spring sprouts a glory of light

Don't talk to me
Yesterday says good-bye
Flows into my mind
A beautiful mirage

So you say I say
Hug me in our loss
I fond you like a day gone by
Whisper of you makes me cry

Plato in the sun under a tree
Seventeen and college
Run away with me now
Before this time slips away

It's too late for you to say hello
Good-bye to all that matters
I wish the best but know
Sorrow's whimsy likely flows.

City Noise

Deaf Pigeons so long ago
Deaf Pigeons with no where to go
Deaf Pigeons what a woeful day
Deaf Pigeons slew me today
Deaf Pigeons

Facade

Please ignore the hole in my gut
The oozing wound
Bent posture
Fatigue
Staggering walk

And the look in my eyes
Vast repository of loss
Wobbled head-borne orbs
Wandering look
Unfocused wellspring
Facial paths carved by the decades

No, I am that which you see
Limber, long and straight
Vibrant and ever ready
Silky movements and calm demeanor
A billboard of charm
On the peeled remnants of time-worn billboards

Underture to 1812 Love

There's a moment when
Your love lifts me
Even when I am far.
Like a distant piano tone
We embrace.
Our dream of each other
Like sustaining water.
Our fluid love taut.
On just ten years knowledge
We have dared
To risk these years
We know are gone.

We good-bye too soon our love
To live like necessary
Syllables in a gone poem
For our generation
Of infant and growing peace.
Amid so many strivings.
Dreaming of warmth
In each other's best
Possible crescendos of our ultimate
Good selves like
White on white

Against dark possibilities
Of our probable mass destiny
As self-centered Nazis
Who love for some state-ordered
Goal of economic

Or social growth that
Makes us pained as
Individuals yet
Still selfish like
Spoiled clarets and
Saddened children too
Aware of death and
Nihilism and
The sad aspect of clowns and
The subservient sickness of animal's low
On the chain rightly named chain and
Limit the order of
Our lives leaning toward
Transcendence we wish
For others and
Sad ourselves to death
With moon and sun and distant
Hope in our eyes like stars
Destined to live forever.

Too True

I've been true to myself yes I have.
Oh, I funk you yes I do
My sibilant spirit soars and attracts.
Everyone says,
"He's the most charismatic man I ever met!"

I know that lake here limits
Me, I'm oceans of dynamic magazine material.
Talk to your friends of my life.
The say, "Wow man."
"Can't believe it."
"Never heard of such greatness."

And not in any negative Nazi way.
No, I'm pure animal magnetism
People attraction
Power driven
Color on gray
Unexpected
Environment transcending.

Say, "Who care 'bout that?"
Only honky-livered Jimmy Olsens
With pathetic hopes of doing the right thing.

I hate those sucker deaths of Vietnam
I hate those married fertile studs trapped
A hoosegow of men with secret handshakes
And lonely dreams of adventure.

That ain't me
And this is my dream!

Doors of Perception

This old lock cannot be opened
The spring is shot
The slot rusted

There is now nothing to protect on the inside
But there you are stuck
Looking at the closed door
Wondering how this happened
Not seeing the riches have long ago fled

Why did you wait so long?
What were you thinking?
When did you plan to act?

Many days will pass in your waiting
Forgetfulness will keep you planted there
When wandering into a new way is your only hope

Walking the Razor's Edge

The sun is always setting
The sun is always rising
Each moment
In the same instant

New life is always emerging
New lives are always passing
Each moment
In the same instant

Light is always creating new space
Light is drawn into blackness
Each moment
In the same instant

Destruction is always creating loss
Creation is always emerging
Each moment
In the same instant

Birth and loss
Loss and birth
This is the dramatic background of our lives

The challenge is to find the glory in each

Growing Up Michigan City

Make your way toward tomorrow
Along the life rope of time
Sing your way to meaning
As the errant country curve crashes towards you at 100 miles per hour
Dave Marciniak says, "Don't worry!" but you know you should
Country roads and too much to drink and smoke
Make midnight dangerous
Will we make this curve?
Is the thrill worth it if we don't?

You cannot follow us
We are moving too fast
Furious and lost
Amid lies and bullshit and uncertainty

Why not risk it all
In a moment of zoom zoom ecstasy
Perhaps rise to the heavens
Perhaps race headlong into the future

We put our disenchanted shoulders to the wheel
As it spins wildly out of control
And calmly light cigarettes
In the dark night of Indiana

The Great Etching Goes On

Where did those days go?
The sunlight and colors cast have all changed
The shadows have grown large in my vision.

Take a look at the distant peaks
They grow close and shallow
My actions move towards a lesser plane

Pause on the pathway
Look back and sigh into the evening's light
Soon you too will be a shadow
Beyond the pale of sun

Fresh breezes will blow
A new moon will rise
Salty sea air will wake others

Bitter cold will lead them
To warm embraces
Great elation will greet them
On a tremendous height

They will see a far shore
A long lament of love lost
A small scratch upon the rock of time

The Mad Way

Sometimes breathing hurts
Moments make you sad
Great cry comes from deep within
A great sobbing in the sky

Loss keeps on happening
In spite of quick movements
Catches up with you

You charge forward bent and shaking
Dream filled with loss and passing
Where will you turn for sustenance?

Perhaps you sacrifice an ear
Or create a great masterpiece
But in the end there is no way
But living through the madness

From the Desk of...

The pulse beat is gray as the office swirls in pastures of limp caresses.
Cheer is raked, burned and spread and spread like ashy fog.

Somewhere inside stands a boarded apparition, gallows-like with a noose of horns hanging westerly, suspended red on the horizon…

The late-night red of resting coal casts shadows that flicker and form vague familiar figures like the silhouettes of faces dreamed long ago.
Out of these faces rises a voice, a sonorous drone, drawing, snakelike yet human.
A rose with petals of fire framed in a halo of deeper red.

Then, a notion to grasp the stem and embrace the flower. Its head moves slowly forward.

Suddenly, boards creak and the earth falls
Leaving only the somnolent stare of eternity resting on a road of feathers—birds that flew.
Then it is lunchtime…

Mirabai Says #2

Grow yourself tall
Be a weed
Spread yourself out
Appear anywhere
In any soil
Need no attention
No nurturing
Distance yourself from sensitivity
Do not be delicate
Hone your ability to adapt
Find strength in foreign lands
Be difficult to eradicate

Do not harbor or cling to false ideas
Do not impose yourself on others
Find your own space
Amid the vast spaces.

Mirabai says teach all to be weeds.

Who Goes There?

I didn't deserve any of their love
Just a faker
Seagulls of madness
On the surface of my depths

Sirens cry on my isolated island
Tired seas lap on my shores
Soft sunlight cloud
Filtered grey illumination

My heart awash with tears
Bitter salt on my tongue
I stand on the sandy shore
My foot on a relic mine

The past a blank explosion
Subdued wound
Seeking surface
Awaiting my patient denial

It is love that is my sin
Given freely and sorely wanted
Splayed against the grindstone of life

Pipers cast sorrow to the winds
Grasping our spirits
Ascending depletion
Refuse rising into a risky sky

The Great Hunt

I have been driven mad by my own white whale
This colossus of my own creation
That can ne'er be seen
Nor ever captured or killed
A jaw-opening threat on the horizon
Looming in the loon of my mind
Baked into my life
Central to my anxiety and motivation
Always lurking there
Just emerging from the deep
And disappearing into the nether of my imagination
The nap and fabric and wave of self

This eminence more grand than life
Shimmers in the watery desert
Nurtured and fed
Housed and sustained
Blunt reality with killer force
The great, the magnificent, the fecund
The feared, the calling, the way

My Bowler Hat

Lies in the fading foliage
Violins play dark and minor
Evil pursuits are uninterrupted

The sea does not know of your troubles
The ephemeral sky does not quiet
It is courage that makes the sun rise

When the seasons pass
Say goodbye with gratitude
Do not grasp the autumn leaf or the summer grass
Let go the spring tulip
And winter frost

Your temporal ways float in a passing breeze
Like white clouds against a pale moon
You will not be happy with your fleeting triumph
Your buffered ego will fall
Your bowler hat will find its way into tatter

The Haunting Shadow

It was romantic in a simple way,
So I yelled it out:
"BLACK!"
It shimmered big in the front seat.
Everyone else got paranoid,
So we left.
On the way black collided hypnotically
Behind Fred's lips.
We drove to the symmetrical woods
Behind the local boy's school.
We cracked sassafras for the smell.
Black receded into the street lamp
On the hill near the house
We always had to avoid.
Later, black rested in the bed post
Where we tossed contraband ashes.
Then, while we listened to whale music,
Black offered up a hand,
Like a wild animal paw,
That snatched at my face
From between my legs.
I recoiled in horror
To have been so betrayed.

Incessant Calling

My broken heart bleeds into clouds
Pots and pans
Clank behind me
Not noises
But dark music of memory

Air roots of the tree grow deep into sky
My yearning like a drop of blood on your cheek
A baby cries alone on a mountain peak
Isolation framed in blue sky

Some things cannot be lifted
Some chasms cannot be crossed
There is nothing between here and there
but vast distance
Vertebrae on the seabed
Fossils in the stone
Scars across my heart.

Let Them Go Their Way

Fathers let your children be
Mothers send them on their way
What great dreams lay seed within their being?
What great heart lies within waiting to emerge?

Beware the façade to sanitize
The fake move to cleanse

This fearsome life
Creates charades of tepid culture
Lifeless activity of fruitless days
A mockery of authenticity
A walking dead
A pre-cursed surrender
A bow to futility
A betrayal of courage
We know this is wrong
And, in our fear we betray our lives.

This loss, this suicidal death
This thin sacrament does not forgive

Let them find their fecund way.

Kingsdoom

Rah, rey, ra, weeeeee
Royalty is great to be
Mai oui you see
Weeeee

Sun king, land king, ding-a-ling king
Bow down and kiss the ring king
What in the world are you thinking king
Do you really have to pull that aristocratic thing?

Divine rights and might makes right
You don't care if you give us a fright
Or run us through or keep us from light
You would just as soon kill us in the night

What are we to you but monkeys in a zoo?
Who are you but someone to rue?
It doesn't matter because in the end we're all screwed

Take your royal chair but beware
We act like we don't care
That we will never share
But we are beyond your stare
In fact, we are everywhere

So be sure to look behind you
Wonder when the real Sun King will find you
Spirit rises to remind you
And the cold dark sting of retribution finds you.

The Lone Ranger Dream

I pick up my
brother's arm put
it on mine my
lifelong mask. I
want to do good
for him, to take
the steps, I'm
supposed to take, on
his arm I promise,
I will
Wear it my eyes
on my purpose a
straight line breaking
through my horizon at
right angles. I start
out from the wrecked
house across from my
home but shortly later
and slowly, my purpose
forgotten, begin to
not look, end up
smiling at a party caught
in that last moment
of anxiety knowing
I have to leave.

Here in the Numb

There it was—nothing
All around me—nothingness
No panorama of blue above
No earthly green
Or black of ground
Or walls or windows or ways
Just nothing

And inside too
A naked blankness
Without misery or angst
No yen to spur
Nor compassion or longing
An unadulterated void

The steady drone
Drumming of the heart
all absent
Missing organs and bloodless veins
No weary bones or tethered tendons

All is quiet
No voice to speak
Words to express
Insight to grasp
Realization to grow
Promise to fulfill

All gone
All simply caught
here in the numb
A captured emptiness
Beyond all sensing

LIVE

Transcending Socialization

We step out of our armor and speak in slow movements of wind
We become gift givers, caretakers of lament

We bury ourselves in earth
Sear ourselves with fire
Cast ourselves into the ocean
Great waves of other and passing crash against our tender figure

We are heroes facing the mysterious and unknown
Waving tiny flags amid strong currents against an empty sky

We are caught in exhaustive competition and a fleeing existence
With dim and limited imaginings and fragile connections to the immense source of life

We are simple peasants spinning an everyday earthly heroism
Through calloused hands
Guiding ourselves through challenge and risk
Ignoring the real dogs of fear that constantly tear at us
Even as we imagine hope

Behind it all, the great skull grins at us while we feast

The billions have passed, shadows in our mind
Turning towards life with bitter looks
And dreams gone by and moments lost
Their messages all that are left
Which we hug to ourselves, treasures to be cherished

Taste the bitter and cherish the sweet
Give up pretense
Turn to those around you
Gather in pale of moon at days end
Laugh and cry and dance together
Free spirits in a celebration of life

Terror's Digest

Just like the butterfly's suicidal dive
From the underpass
Towards the windshield
To the surf swoop
On the airwave
Followed by a lazy curtsy
In the rearview
I'll swallow my terror.

I'll feel its edge
Touch, fondle, digest,
Growl and roar in it.
I'll punch and mold it
Until it feeds cake and ice cream to the insects.

I will bounce and roll it out to the trash
Cover it with old spinach cans
Leftover spaghetti
Wet cardboard
And kitty litter waste.

I'll lock it in the garbage can
Roll it over jagged rocks
That rip and pull like animated monsters.
I'll kick it straight and true
Over the rushingest waterfall
This side of the moon.
Then I will turn on the light.

Out on a Limb

My heart twists in the breeze
like the grizzled heavy body
of a Western hung man—vigil ante dead.
Tick tock human pendulum

keeping time to spinning earth
and hopeful looking as a young prostitute,
a sad, pathetic innocence reeking
limited horizons and short sightedness.

Whole world drives
by in a big fancy car
no one can slow down to give me the low down.
In youth our hearts hang ripe

like fragrant fruit on limbs
Whispering midsummer's night enchantment
intoxicating, expectation, opportunity!
Yahooing out our firm aortas

dancing cha cha cha and swaying
with romance on breezy limbs
We seek each other
reacting to other like

diversion that is movement
finding voice that says we
not I but yet I say we

I open my heart though it's beat
and float, like a feathery child, adrift on a wave
of golden light: another young heart gone autumnal
Taking my chances.

Old Heart and Soul

The stupidity of my hand,
The moving shadow of auto,
Illumes my midnight sanctuary.
Quiet reigns against my will,
A dictator in my house.
You and I communicate
In veiled assumptions
Of what we want.

My soul,
Lost in a cultured cave,
Refined out of existence.
My nails manicured
To perfection
My spirit
Jagged as static.

Put your ear to my belly.
Hear the motion of my organs.
My life makes
My beast a tenor,
An intellectual dancer
With the sexuality
Of an office desk.
Speak to me in new words.
Grow new organs of excitement.
Let's rub hair in ecstasy
Form a new kingdom of abandonment.
Grasp the loneliness of my cells.
Feel the motion of my useless growth.
Know the screams of my ancestors lost in the forest.

Freewheelin'

There's a life in me want out.
I don't care what no folk say.
There's a restless life jitterbug free
Full a' hard livin' and sweet grindin'...
Fluid, loose, resourceful, "don't-give-a-shit,"
Wild, edge-of-night, long-lovin',
Scared-of-nuthin', hobo-ridin', girl-chasin',
Barrier-breakin' life in me want out.
Now! Wants out! Life in me want out!
No lynch mob
Sedentary pale spirits
Gonna stop me now...
I'm free. I'm wild. I'm proud.
I'm ruby red love.
I'm the life I always wanted to be.
Ready for you. Ready for anything.
I'm gonna strut my free-wheelin' stuff
Down funky Broadway. Gonna
Go-man-go blue-night ultra-sax smooth
Sound like panther-after-prey prowl
Through rich night of smoky magic and rare blue feelings.
I'm gonna flaunt my living self and fast talk you all.
I'm jungle happy and hip.
I'm free. I'm wild. I'm proud.
Ready for you. Ready for anything.
I'm skybound and full of a thousand sons...
Generations of hard lovers dedicated to full life.
No turn on the video till you die for me or my kin.
We are full. We are flesh. We are free. We are proud.
We are gold in a leaden world.

We are pure unprocessed bubblin' burnin'
Hot soft-shufflin' cool too ram roddin' hunks of pure funk
Shinin' stars in a dark night...ragin'
Ready for you. Ready for anything.

Waiting for Wings

I feel like Humphrey Bogart
beat up
drugged
stinking of boredom and pain
emotions like five o'clock shadow
on the sensitive sole of my sore spirit
nagging like a rotten cold—
a jagged cough like a long-repressed urge
gathering at the mouth of my restraints
waiting for a world-wide hug.

Six billion people grown warm
and ready for an embrace…
a cold washcloth to the international forehead
like a sentimental song from the early 1960's
perhaps *"I Need Your Love."*

Or a sumptuous and powerful sea
that releases our alien spirit
once bound in our emasculated revolt
grasped by the scientific equation of time and space.

Not like our two heartbeats,
pressed like bird's wings
reaching through a cage
with storybook momentum
a spontaneous dance of two bodies
feeling their nerves sing alive.

"I'll come any minute."
You're a great suggestive flirt
like cool air on my genitals
or lady with a spotlight behind her white dress
with thick-lipped smile and joyous hand clapping,
jiggerous and penis straitening alley-cat groans
liberating as a summer night.

You a lovely illusion like an angora sweater
on a high school cheerleader,
or heavy lipstick on a girl from the wrong side.
Oh you!
The image at the height of a masturbatory dream...

A violin makes you remember time
and imagine wings on the sensation of body
that reminds you you'll lay still someday,
like the Romans,
become dusty like the ancient Greek,
and forget these fake smiles.

Hollow Reeds

On this day the light shimmers
The summer air easy

He writes messages of warning
On old brown pants
Leaves them unsecured
On sidewalks at the edge of town

What happens when the storm comes?
A great wind blows through
Each of us and all things
A great sound rises

What music are you playing?

Shimmer Me Timbers

When we go a walking where
The wild winds do blow
There we find ourselves among
The dark woods shadowy flow

In trance and trend we vie and fend
The snake its withering stare
Wends its way through thick and thin
These twins all hearts must bear

And hear we there without a care
The fleece sounds shimmer and glow
Gold light does shine o'er yours and mine
That's if you see it so

So don't you think it wise to wink
Though hearts may sink so low
You'll see you'll find it oh so sweet
Twinkling smiles into the flow

I Raise My Hand in Celebration

I raise my hand in celebration
In protest
In physical revelation
Long sinews of arm stretched in the delight of movement

This life
This chance for amazement
Infinite awe of cloud formations
Leaf and wind in movement
Scattered beauty
The resplendency of natural chaos revealed

The wild whistle of the free bird
The thin thistle blossom
Agencies of the senses to absorb
Mind to process
Soul to rise

Transcend the overtly criminal and subtle gravities
Of politics and religion
These false manifestations
Distractions from miracle
Life abasements
Sour sorrows of life

But keep the pedal down on enlightenment
Keep that hand raised
Palm open
Eyes wide with hope

As You Walk the Curved and Crooked Way

There is perfection in the isosceles triangle
Solid foundation
Arrow to the sky

But we are all soft edged
Bent toward earth
Hooped and questioning
Caved and distant from ideal form
Time is our Master

So bear witness
Fire up the darkness
Cast long shadows
Create art and poetry
Make music, dance
As you walk the curved and crooked way

Way of the Gambler

Hold your hands high
The future is pointing a gun at you
The Wild West of your heart says draw

The restless wind bounces round your brain
Tumbleweed of desire and passing
There is no giving up

The wind will sweep you forward
You must walk the dodgy path
Stumble towards the horizon like fallen leaves

Your trail leaves little scent
Swift flowing river washes your way
Your destination lies in the Western sun
All cards inevitably on the table

Let Go the Sentries of Your Heart

Let go the sentries of your heart
Release wild into the dank prison
Let wild birds flutter their way skyward

Your bedraggled horse looks weary
Lame from stumbling
That giant windmill tries to pierce your heart

No matter as castle walls crumble
There is no possibility of retreat
Only acceptance will serve the day

Tilt your lance skyward
Toward a target that cannot be hit
Be happy in the effort

Equine Surprise

There is a blue horse in the forest
You wake and ride into the sunrise
Bright sun imbues your youthful spirit
A freedom that cannot be repeated

This is a story you later doubt
Hard to remember this energy
Or the liberating gallop into the light

What wild wakes you now
Sends you zooming through the dew
Away to new horizons
And the coming of a colorful tomorrow?

Heartbeat Mystery

Much sand between here and the ocean
Wilds of Africa stir my soul
Hyena in me loves the moon

I cannot reach the sky with my hand
Moon is too high to grasp
Stars invigorate my vision
Milky Way fills my eyes

The path to the sea is blocked with distraction
Thousands of new moons darken the horizon
Sun sparkles and pulse goes silent

Wake into a night of tall trees and deep roots
A horizon that lasts forever
The tide comes in and you are on your way

Don't explain it's not your fault
There is just mystery in your heartbeat

To Breathe Divine

The compass jibe
The ocean's swell
The four wind's blistering blow

Winter winds cry
An icy breath's sigh
Cold that bites your heart

To reach is whimsy
To stretch absurd
To bluster simply vain

Though shadow falls
On darkened times
Rising sun all wrong

Still light is cast
Expanse is vast
Make your heart grow strong

Then birds do sing
Sweet melody rings
Tunes from nature spring

The said is said
The laughter bled
Your precious time extended

Be glad for your days
Like shimmering waves
Casting their lot to the shore

Portents

Seven swans emerge from white cloud in a blue sky
Seven crows perch on the black limbs of a dead elm
No wonder your anxious walk

Toss and turn in a thin night
Horizon loud with shrieking birds
Lightening in the distance
Thunder in the sky

Rain falls on the dry seeds of your life
Loud with the cracking of shell and shoot
Harsh pain of a delicate tendril reaching
As new life stretches for light.

Winter's Way

I would leave this broken house
Were it not overgrown with tender branches
White with snow
In chill winter wind

Thorny bramble wrapped in ice
Cold winter sun shines
Warm enough for moist glist'ning.

A dark twilight moon
Dim light cast on fleeing clouds
On their way to nowhere in particular

Outside a seagull soars
White on white against the winter snow
Seeking sustenance
Swelling waters bound by ice

One day I will join them
In their search for the sea

Opportunity

There is a moment soft and pliable
Just ahead
Ready to be molded and forged
On the eternal fire of ever-passing time
Attuned to what matters

The swoop of the seagull
The tra-la-la of the morning bird
The feathery touch of cloud moist in a resonant blue sky.

Billions and trillions
Or infinite moments of creation
Each culminating now
Full of dimension and wonder beyond perspective

Grown for you to join with this given procession
Inspired to find meaning
Which was made for you
And that will forever be lost
Should you decide to turn away
And meander on your own lost roads
Where the distant moon does not reverberate with life
And the moist dark earth and fertile forest
Fall in an instant
Turning into harsh sand and brown leaves
Absent of night and the wild cooing of day

Do not miss the invisible hand to show the way
It will be here and gone
And its soft touch can be like a moment gone
Or a vision created.

Salvation Way

When the sand rises
When the moon falls
When your heart grows dim

The horizon you see cannot be reached in wisdom
The dance you feel in your bones cannot be realized
There is a shortness in your body that reaches into your soul

This is sadness better not seen
A dark way beyond the vision of your heart
A place of fear where your pulse races

Abandon ship and sink into the unknown
There is a current of salvation
Like a frightening wave you must ride

Wayward Heart

It's only later you will know
Your heart vessel hard and splintered as old bamboo.
Yes, a bitter root will grow where your love should be.
You will vibrate in a yawning empty space

This is not the way
The current blows the flotsam clean

Green shoots find their way
Past boulders and gravity
Towards the sun

Wake up to an emanating energy
That comes from deep within you
And flies like light
Towards the edge of a dark universe
Saying, "Yes."

TRANSIENCE

There We Are Gone

I

I should have put to writing
So much that has been forgotten
Sacred moments
Now only dimly echo in autumn memory.

Winter wakes
Steward of the cold
As wispy snow blows
Fine and cold against the cheek.

The moment at dawn
On the beach
With your child asleep in the tent
And Lake Michigan glowing red

So many hundreds of birds
Flying over colored trees
Restless as time and just as fleeting

The few moments of calm
Like brilliant flashes
Amid the onslaught
Of another day

II

Pouring rain on rooftop
Flashing light through window
Into the peace of your rest
Pre-dawn walks
On summer nights

III
When long shadows pour
Across the landscape
And fade into night

When it is you
And your surroundings
And quiet crashes
Against your being

When cold creeps down
Into your bones
And your vulnerability leaps

IV
These kingdoms that fashion themselves
And in a moment are gone

We must savor
We must reflect
We must appreciate
We must honor
We must share

Look at me now
And loose yourself
In the dream

Look at us shine
Look at us urge the world
See us pass like a wave of light

In Memory of Epiphany

The song sprang from my heart
Like all songs do
Just in the moment it comes
Like all inspiration

Here we are and then we are gone
Words flutter in the breeze
Shoot into space
Indecipherable to the stars

We imagine we are broken
But our hearts beat steady rhythm
Our actions melody
Mellifluous and sacred as thought

You love our love a kiss
Your moist warmth meets me in time
And then is memory of us
Lost and gone but here in my mind

This vibration lives in me
Blasts through my defenses like moon from clouds
Lives in my heart
Like a blood that flows in rivers

Wakes me in memory
A sea of passing
That beats in a wild rush
Of everlasting longing

Cells of tenderness
A humanness amid the mechanical passing of time
A magic moment that lasts
As we all move on.

After Reading *Night* by Elie Wiesel

One spent raindrop life
Conscious of writing
A window hieroglyph.

Vegetarian Love Sick Blues

Roses spring red from my body
My veins green vines and thorns
Sweet scent attracts joy seekers
My head full of wounded birds

Petals pucker with hunger
Come sweet things of the sunshine
Kiss my aromatic lips
Do not go hungry
Feed yourself upon me
As I you
And we
Sustain for a moment
In the heat of the sun
And cool of evening
Amid long days of summer
Alive together all of us
Until the cold frost of winter
Lays us to rest.

And It Is All Just A Passing

Royal thrones and castles high
The smooth and soft way of your thigh
Restless wind and shimmering sea
Everything you'll ever be

And it's all just a passing

Desert Storm and starving sighs
The day that you said your last goodbye
Murderous troops and sad torture
Makes it hard to find true rapture

And it's all just a passing

There's the leaf, there's the tree
A falling away has got to be
The yellow sun and blue sky
The moon with clouds swiftly by

And it's all just a passing

Don't put yourself in a particular place
Keep your eye on a subtle grace
See the sea move in and out
Constant movement all about

And it's all just a passing
And it's all just a passing

Transience

White stars shine as bones
Ashen ancient lights
Tethered by nothing
Suspended and skeletal.

Bright body of sky shines
On decayed yellow tree
Flowers purple with mercy
Blossoms of dusty wandering
Holiness grows ripe
God turns his head to harvest
Leaving seedy haloes of promise.

We travel our rootless ways
Wicks of fire as we move.

Autumn's Frost

When the night is pitch black
Time just returned to Standard
Monday night dark
So dense with streetlights glowing bright
Tarmac reflective with soft rain and mist
Brisk blows the wind
Trees shorn of many leaves
Rasping last breaths of autumn

Breathe deep the quick turn of season
The cold sharp visible breath
Quiet night and warm furnace
See it go
See the never ending movement

It wakes up my cells
My senses snort with life
Big energy vibrates
With life passing in the cold
Of a fall breeze gone

Cicada Brigadoon

The cicadas rise
Seek light and height
Drunk with urges
Staggering flight

Sweet primal fornication
Wild with life
A Woodstock Nation
Communal their song

Dancing and naked
Thousands swarming up
To impregnate and descend
Their joyous pronouncements fulfilled.

Continuation

Can't count on it
May not happen
Could be
Look out for tomorrow

Monkey's glee in the cinnamon tree
Neanderthal eyes under a starry sky
Tick tock gone
Times great wrong
Most murderous throng
Seconds ticking on

What buffaloes roam
What waters foam
There is no steady home
Just moving on

What lost ecstasy
To think you will no longer be
As far as the eye can see

There are bars
There are stars
So many viscous claws
Ways of acting beyond all laws

Look up into a blue sky
There the only promise lies
Skyscapes to suss
Horizons above loss
Life without a cross

Daze of Cain

I miss those days
When young birds flew across oceans
When your heart said flight
Red waves in the sunset

The sweet aroma of orchids
Overcame your loss
Sweet apples yours for the plucking
This is why you tarried so long

Travel to Nod
And let your murder go
Do not speak of it
The wind blows fresh ideas to the heavens

We embrace in this place we are exiled
Warm rivers flow and touch each other
For the moment we are secure

Lost wings and feathers fly like autumn leaves
We too are taken by the wind
Traveling to a place
Beyond our purpose

What's that I see?
Blue waters?

Fly By Night

only a poem will tell
how awful I feel
on my tiptoes
reaching for a puffy
cloud cloud cloud...

white and buoyant
full of floating
I escape
like a saintly dirigible
for a tired
body body body...

romantic mental longings
seek to find
physical exchange
as dynamic as the moment
you open your eyes
wide
and see your spirit dart into darkness

Either Way Gone

The wrought iron of the lamp painted gold
Trumped by wild horses galloping in the night outside your window

The air inside is tight, the light dim
The promise of the shadows is lost in an uncertain future

The sound of the wind, melodic and enchanting
Cannot be heard above the noise racing around these cramped quarters

Dream of empty rooms just daring you to go there
Alive but frightening in their absence of light, their billowing darkness

The promise of tomorrow filled with the horror of mystery
The invigorating presence of life with its unceasing passing and loss

The joy that is this moment now fills us
And leaves us empty, searching in the funnel for a new glow

Lightening amid the storm
Open the windows, feel the rain on your brow

Hear the mad stomping of the running horses
Listen to the wind gone mad as you rise in the ether and are away.

Embrace the Moment

Don't say no to me
On this twisting road
Say yes to this moment in time
It is ours for the taking

Why don't you look at me
As this moment passes
There is snow in a future of cold
Your warm heart beats against the present

With you the heights create my horizon
Top of the world mountain says touch me
Tall visions of warmth seek our day
Find me as I find you, alive in the moment

Sweet smile like a youthful love
Unencumbered by swift passing
Your youth makes me love
We reach toward each other and are gone.

Harpbreak Hotel

Bits of the past
Loaded with feeling
A few measures of sad string music
A still life painting
Ruddy faces and dogs in medieval decadence
The pale face of time embalmed in our minds
Who knows the many millions of sadnesses
The untold loneliness
The last moments of regret
Who can say where we will end
Lifeless and staring
Heaven on our minds

The Joining

I give myself to the wind and the grass
Send all sparks skyward
The stars luxuriate in my essence

I breathe in the dust of my ancestors
Exhale their storms and passions
Fierce longings and unfulfilled dreams
They play upon the landscape and are lost

Our energies meet on the vanishing point
In the deep perspective of passing
In the heartbreak beyond seeing
In the last moments of awareness
That take your breath away

The Great Getaway

like some misshapen rock,
one grotesque igneous totem face,
separate.
a sensitive Neanderthal,
a clumsy disturbance moving through disturbance.
a fountain of tears bursting from a stone.

you hold me in your grand wet father hands
to examine.
you think how odd my shape,
how hopeless the ugliness
of something so beautiful gone bad.
you turn away.

the summer sun sinks low and red
into a river sky.
dirtied with dusty waterside gravel
the wish to immerse silently
into the wet horizon.
to merge and float seaward.
to emerge clean into wide seas of eternity.

The Long and Short of It

There is just straight madness in manifestations
There is just straight joy
You decide
Or not

Why don't you take the sun into your hands
Or swallow the moon
These things are just as impossible

No church can contain my spirit
No horizon dampens my heart
The arc of my growth bigger than any orbit

My finger is a blot against the sky
But my heart rises with the sun
Pulses red into a morning sky

New Year's Midnight with *Look Homeward Angel*

1993 lunges into an old story
Like a ukulele solo during a rock concert.
Gant dying, Ben dying

Little child, meaty, cold day, raised hand.
Unfeeling and dull eye, unswitched spirit,
All active cells banned, programmed decay
Of skin we loved, quiet, absent energy.
Wolfe eyes!

Ben, your little heart leapt last hurdle of night
That moment of first imagined death awareness
Which with criminals casts our lot,
        Makes might
Vanity, a power sure to possess.

Everlasting death for all who rise
Who stand frail heart, perhaps unrecognized,
And shout our dreams to the stars
Hope our image lasts, our fortune read
By those in whom we live though we are dead.

Playground of Silence

Classmates fall like raindrops from the sky
Upon this old heart
Sad with so much missing

Bright eager and innocent eyes
Not dulled by nunnery suppression
But rebellious spirits
Armed with creepy crawlers and spitballs
Bucking Broncos of youth

Sixty years later I mourn their faded ways
These school mates of time
Resonate stories of twinkled youth
Fates cast into myriad morrows
Carved into wandering paths
Lost
But bonded by memory
Deep in the warm rooms of the soul
Amid this classroom of empty desks

Made in the USA
Monee, IL
15 April 2023

31919575R00204